The sky had cleared at last, baby blue with white cloud masses near the horizon, and the sun was warm. The tide was ebbing strongly. Wycliffe walked on the sleepers like a schoolboy. After the coal-yard, the timber-yard, surrounded by a high fence. Here the family declared itself: Bryce Brothers, Timber and Builders' Merchants. A circular saw screamed tormentedly. Beyond the timber-yard a well-maintained town; the wharf petered out but the railway track continued, running under the trees by the river. On a bend, a quarter of a mile farther upstream, he could see the little station, the terminus for passenger traffic. The trees were part of an estate and a little way along the road Wycliffe could see impressive gate posts and a drive entrance. This must be Boslow.

Matthew Bryce's wife had been found in the river.

W.J. Burley lived near Newquay in Cornwall, and was a schoolmaster until he retired to concentrate on his writing. His many Wycliffe books include, most recently, *Wycliffe and the Guild of Nine*. He died in 2002.

Wycliffe
AND THE
GUILT EDGED ALIBI

W.J.Burley

An Orion paperback

First published in Great Britain in 1971
by Victor Gollancz Ltd
under the title *Guilt Edged*
First published in paperback in 1974
by Arrow
This paperback edition published in 2006
by Orion Books Ltd,
Orion House, 5 Upper St Martin's Lane,
London WC2H 9EA

1 3 5 7 9 10 8 6 4 2

A CIP catalogue record for this book is available
from the British Library.

ISBN-13 978-0-7528-8083-9
ISBN-10 0-7528-8083-7

Printed and bound in Great Britain by
Clays Ltd, St Ives plc

The Orion Publishing Group's policy is to use papers that
are natural, renewable and recyclable products and
made from wood grown in sustainable forests. The logging
and manufacturing processes are expected to conform to
the environmental regulations of the country of origin.

www.orionbooks.co.uk

I

The estuary of the Treen River divides East from West Treen, but the two are linked by a car and passenger ferry, a floating platform with a ramp at each end and a hut-like superstructure on each side. The hut on one side houses the diesel engine and the one on the other provides shelter for foot passengers when it rains. The engine drives sprocket wheels which, as they rotate, pick up a pair of chains from the bed of the river and haul the craft from shore to shore and back again. Sailings are at half-hour intervals from June to August inclusive, but less frequent at other times. By the third week in September business was already slack, and at ten-thirty on Tuesday morning the skipper and his mate had made only two return trips, one for the workers at seven-thirty and one for the white-collars at eight-thirty. Now they were taking aboard the milk lorry on its way back to the factory after the morning collection from farms on the east side. Apart from the lorry there was a private car, a Cortina 1600, driven by a smooth-faced young fellow who probably sold soap. The lorry clanked up the ramp, rattling the timber treads, lurched along the length of the deck and came to a halt, its near-side wing almost touching the steel plates of the chain-chute and its radiator an inch or two from the safety gates. The driver, like all regulars, prided himself on occupying the minimum of space even though at this time of year he usually had the ferry to himself. The Cortina revved and skidded on the slimy ramp, ending up in the middle of the deck space where there should have been room for a dozen like him. The driver looked bored and lit a cigarette.

Dickie Bray, mate on the ferry for thirty-eight years, was a hunch-back with spindly bowed legs, but agile as an ape so that the economy of his movement was a joy to watch. He did everything except drive the engine, which was the job of the skipper who rarely left his noisy, smelly little hut. Dickie closed the landward gates, operated the great spoked wheel which raised the ramp, then with a desultory wave of the hand, gave the skipper 'the off'. The ferry drew smoothly, almost imperceptibly away from the shore. Dickie collected a fare from the soap salesman then joined his friend the lorry driver at the seaward gates. The milk factory paid by the month. The two men filled and lit their pipes and stood, arms on the gates, staring at the silver grey water just ahead of where the chains broke surface. The tide was flowing strongly, eddying round the clumsy craft and pushing her broadside upstream against the chains. The shiny peak of Dickie's cap seemed to obscure his vision but he was the first to spot the body bobbing about in the track of the port chain. Often the chains disturbed mysterious debris on the bottom, sending it up for a few seconds of turbulent surface life, but this was different: a brown bundle of clothes, the material bellied out by water like a parachute. Dickie gave a screech like a startled gull, the signal for an emergency stop; the engine died at once and the chains ceased to rattle through the chute. The bundle bobbed alongside, kept there by the flow of the tide. Dickie went over the gate on to the ramp and began fishing with a boathook; the skipper came out of his cabin and lowered the ramp until it was awash and Dickie could land his catch. A smooth operation, all over in less than a minute. The soap salesman got out of his car and joined the little group around the bundle which proved to be the body of a woman.

She lay on the boards in a pool of water. Her posture was stiff though credibly life-like, but her face was pallid, gnawed and leprous. The salesman went quickly back to the deck leaving the other three staring down at her. The ferrymen had fished several out of the estuary, dead or alive but mostly dead, and the lorry driver had a strong stomach. It was impossible to tell from her face but her figure was that of a young woman, small and well proportioned. She wore a brown two-piece with what seemed to be a pink blouse. Her shoes were dainty and fashionable. Her hair was black like a Spaniard's but in whatever style she had worn it, now it splayed lankly on the timbers. There was a necklace of amber beads round her throat and she wore a wedding ring, half buried in the sodden flesh of her finger.

The skipper, a little man with shiny brown cheeks like a hazel-nut, was sparing of words. He looked at his mate and a silent message must have passed. Dickie nodded, 'I thought so too.'

The lorry driver looked at both of them. 'Who is she?'

Dickie straightened himself and glanced vaguely in the direction of the west bank where the other half of the town sprawled raggedly up the hillside. 'I reckon it's Mrs Bryce – Matt's wife.'

The lorry driver whistled.

Dickie took his pipe, half smoked, from his pocket, looked at it and put it away again. The skipper said unexpectedly, 'Death is no respecter of persons.' He was a chapel man.

Without another word, as though working to a well rehearsed drill, the skipper and Dickie lifted the body and carried it into the passenger hut where they laid it on the slatted wooden seat and covered it with a tarpaulin. Water dripped through the slats to form a pool on the floor. Then they got moving again and in a few minutes the ferry was nudging the cobbled slipway on the western side. Dickie lowered the ramp while the skipper went over to the soap salesman. 'You'd best wait . . .' He nodded towards the little hut where the body was. 'I expect they'll want a word . . .'

Dickie was off up over the cobbles on to the wharf, lolloping along close to the houses, like a chimpanzee. The lorry driver climbed back into his cab and re-lit his pipe.

The slipway cut into the wharf at a steep angle so that the ferry was largely hidden except to anyone actually passing by; but there was nobody about. A few yards upstream was the boatyard, dominated by a huge corrugated iron shed, rusting in attractive browns and oranges and reds, like encrusted lichens. Just downstream was the car-park, given over for the week to a fair with dodgems, roundabouts, booths and stalls. But at this time of day it was shrouded in striped canvas.

The sun shone out of a watery blue sky, the breeze was fresh and the tide lapped and chuckled round the ferry. A baker's van cruised slowly along the wharf but the driver appeared to notice nothing. The church clock chimed and struck eleven.

Another ten minutes went by before a small blue and white police car came down the slipway and pulled up just short of the ramp. A uniformed constable got

8

out, followed by Dickie Bray. The constable came aboard, walked over to the entrance to the passenger hut, peered inside, then placed himself on guard at the door. Dickie joined the skipper in the engine room to share a flask of lukewarm black tea. 'The sergeant's fetching Dr Greenly.'

The skipper nodded.

It was a quarter of an hour later that Sergeant Penrose and Dr Greenly arrived and by that time a few quay loafers had gathered at the top of the slipway. Dr Greenly, the police surgeon, was self-important, red-haired, red-faced, and irritated by this interruption to his rounds. The sergeant came across to the engine house, leaving the doctor with the body. 'Just the bare facts; there'll be statements later.'

The salesman got out of his car and came over. 'Is it all right for me to shove off? I'm losing business.'

'That will be in order, sir. Just identify yourself to the constable and tell him where you can be reached.'

The lorry driver, too, was sent on his way.

When Dr Greenly came out of the passenger hut he seemed worried rather than irritated. 'You know who you've got in there?'

The sergeant nodded. 'Apparently it's Mrs Bryce.'

'It is.'

'The point is, Doctor . . .'

'The point is, Sergeant, that I'm not satisfied Mrs Bryce's death was due to drowning.'

'You don't think . . . ?'

Greenly cut him short. 'I don't think anything at the moment except that you should get in touch with your inspector. In cases of prolonged immersion speed is important if the cause of death is to be correctly determined.'

Pompous old fool! But Penrose knew the signs; this

was going to be one of those cases where everybody is anxious to get out from under. The sister of a former cabinet minister and prominent front bench politician. 'I'll radio Information room at once, Doctor.'

He had to drive his car up on to the wharf before he could raise Information Room on his radio but when he succeeded their response was prompt. In five minutes he had his instructions. Inspector Harker of Divisional CID was on his way. He would notify relatives and make arrangements for formal identification. No room for blundering sergeants in this exercise! And a suitable vehicle would be sent to transport the body to the pathologist's laboratory at the county hospital. The goods to be delivered in a plain van.

All the same it was after midday before Detective Superintendent Wycliffe, head of Area CID, heard of the crime.

The Area Crime Squad is not housed in the new police headquarters on the outskirts of the city but tucked away in a Queen Anne house in a secluded crescent near the cathedral. The other houses in the crescent are used as offices by the diocesan authorities who, nearly thirty years ago, had leased one of their houses to the now extinct city force as temporary premises after the bombing. The chief superintendent's offices on the first floor include a large, finely proportioned room with a heavily decorated plaster ceiling which catches dust and houses spiders. The two tall sash-windows overlook a small public garden laid out round a fragment of the old city wall and, beyond that, a modern shopping precinct.

Wycliffe was sitting at his desk reading and making notes from a book entitled *Psychopathic Aggression* written by a gentleman with an unpronounceable Polish name. He had had time for such things recently for business was slack. The notes on his pad were cryptic but, as he would probably never look at them again, this scarcely mattered.

'The psychopath is never a depressive; his hatred is always untroubled by feelings of guilt . . .

'The psychopath appears to be wholly indifferent to the opinions of others, even to their manifest and threatening hostility . . .'

The page was covered by his ragged and rather clumsy script and there were half-a-dozen such mutilated extracts. During every slack period he promised himself that he would catch up on his reading and he would accumulate a little sheaf of notes which would go into a drawer at the first telephone call and into the waste paper basket when he came across them a month later. The present lull had lasted longer than usual and it seemed that, with the tourist season over, crooks as well as landladies and hotel keepers had gone to Majorca for their holidays. But for him it ended with a call on his private line from headquarters. He picked up the telephone.

'Wycliffe.'

'Ah, Charles! I wondered if I might catch you.' It was Bellings, the assistant chief, suave and a master of double talk. No love lost between the two men. 'This is a delicate matter, Charles, probably a mare's nest but there has to be an investigation. We must try not to tread on anybody's toes.'

Wycliffe let him run on. It was the sort of situation Bellings enjoyed: at heart he was a politician rather than a policeman.

'You know Treen? A little watering place and a bit of a port . . . The Bryces are big people there, they own the harbour installations, the timber-yard, the canning factory, the coal-yard and half the town . . . Clement Morley, the former Minister of State, is a brother-in-law . . . You see . . . ? What?' A cultured laugh.

Wycliffe had not spoken a word; he was trying to light his pipe while holding the telephone to his ear with his shoulder.

'There's nobody with you?'

'No.'

'Good! His wife has been found drowned.'

'Whose wife? Morley's?'

'No, my dear chap, Bryce's. Actually there are three brothers and this is the wife of the eldest – Matthew, the head of the clan. She is Clement Morley's sister.'

'And it's a job for us?'

'Well, that's the point. The police surgeon isn't too happy and the body has been sent to Franks, the pathologist . . . We shall know better how to proceed when we have his report . . . On the other hand . . .' Bellings left the unfinished sentence hanging in the air. Unfinished sentences were part of his stock-in-trade. 'My wife and I have met the lady socially. Unstable, neurotic . . . One wouldn't be too surprised to hear that she had . . . You get my meaning . . . ? And Charles, there's quite a bit of gossip about another man, but we don't want to make too much of it unless it's strictly relevant . . .' Bellings' voice drifted away into silence but he hadn't yet made his point to his entire satisfaction. 'You appreciate, Charles, that she is Morley's sister, so we can't afford to have a . . . a cock-up.' The vulgarity was exquisitely enunciated. One had the impression that he had learned a certain number of such expressions for use in dealing with his social inferiors although, as

Wycliffe knew, his father had been a taxi driver. 'The Chief feels that your experience and tact . . . This fellow Morley has a reputation as a head hunter . . .'

'I know him,' Wycliffe growled, and immediately regretted it.

'Socially?'

'You could say that.'

Bellings purred. 'Well, that's splendid! A weight off my mind. By the way, Charles, Treen is not a bad little place – book in at the Manor Park; they do you very well there . . .'

When Bellings rang off, Wycliffe asked to be put through to Franks, the County Pathologist. They had worked together before. But, as he expected, it was much too early for any news. Franks promised to ring the police station at Treen as soon as he was ready with a preliminary report. As there was no point in starting a full scale investigation without more to go on, Wycliffe felt justified in taking a look round on his own.

At one o'clock he was joining the west bound traffic out of the city at the start of his seventy mile drive to Treen. As though to mark the end of his inaction the weather had undergone an abrupt change. Blue-black clouds which had swiftly climbed up the sky from the south east now blotted out the sun, and it was raining. By the time he had cleared the suburbs he seemed to be in the middle of a cloud-burst. All the cars had their lights on and they were swishing through a surface film of water which could not drain away fast enough, sending up bow waves of muddy spray. The windscreen wipers thudded monotonously and inadequately.

Wycliffe, a cautious, perhaps a nervous driver, knew that he would hate every mile of the journey. Although

13

the first fury of the rain storm soon spent itself there was no sign of it stopping and it was almost three o'clock before he could leave the grey stream of lorries and cars on the main road for the eight miles of country lanes which led to Treen. The final approach to the town is down a one-in-six hill with cunning twists, except for the last quarter-of-a-mile which runs straight and steep between two rows of terraced houses propping each other up against the slope.

The principal shops of the town are grouped round a cobbled square with the war memorial in the middle, but the life of West Treen is on its waterfront, strung out along half-a-mile of the west bank of the estuary from the railway station to the harbour. The timber-yard, the coal-yard, the fish canning factory on the site of the old ice works, a boatyard, the ferry slipway, then the slipway, then the harbour with its pubs, cafés and souvenir shops. Beyond the harbour a few bungalows, then National Trust property to Trecarne Head.

Wycliffe parked in the square which was almost deserted. The rain had eased to a drizzle but the cobbles were still running with water and a drain at the lower side of the square was choked so that a pool of brown, muddy water had formed, covering the pavement and threatening nearby shops. A man, his head and shoulders draped with a sack, stood, up to his ankles in the water, prodding listlessly with a stick.

A short, narrow street opened on to the harbour and Wycliffe had his first view of the estuary. There was little colour in the scene but he liked the place on sight. Across the narrow strip of water, opposite where he stood, was the other half of the town, a huddle of grey, slate-roofed houses, but elsewhere the fields and little patches of woodland came almost down to the water, separated from it by a few feet of rocks and shingle. Away to his right, between the two headlands, he could glimpse the distant horizon of the sea. Nearby most of the cafés and shops were closed, some of them boarded up for the winter. It was half-tide and three or four faded blue fishing boats neatly matched their reflections in the still waters of the basin. He came to a large, ugly house with several gables and pebble-dashed walls. It had a wooden verandah built out over the wharf with seats underneath where half-a-dozen men in blue jerseys and peaked caps smoked in silence. Gilded, cut-out letters, fixed to the verandah rail, read: 'Treen Hotel. Tourist and Commercial'.

A mile or so out of the town he had noticed an impressive drive entrance with an arched sign above it: 'Manor Park Hotel'. No doubt it adjoined the golf course and no doubt it was in or trying to get into the pages of *The Good Food Guide*. Wycliffe liked good food but he felt that the hotel on the wharf would be nearer to the realities of life in Treen. He pushed open the glass swing doors of the entrance and found himself in a dimly lit lobby, deserted but for a giant marmalade cat curled up on the reception desk. The bell was answered by a girl who came out wiping her hands on a kitchen cloth. Wycliffe asked her for a room which opened on to the verandah and got one without difficulty. 'There is no-one almost, now that the season is over . . .' She was foreign, Swedish, he guessed, very fair and aggressively healthy, with rather too much bosom and self-confidence for the average English male.

'You want to eat tonight?'

He understood that the question referred to dinner and said that he did.

'Then it is mix grill or salad.'

He nodded, 'That will do.'

She frowned with impatience. 'Which?'

'Oh, the mixed grill.' He was a mug, always falling for the idea of lamb's liver, kidneys and mushrooms, when experience told him that he would get sausage and bacon with a slice or two of greasy tomato.

'Seven o'clock, then.'

'Is there any chance of something to eat now?'

'The kitchen is closed.'

'All right, I'll bring my car round.'

She prodded the air with her ball-point. 'After you have sign the register.'

Outside the rain had stopped and watery sunshine was transforming the field across the water from olive to lime green. He fetched his car from the square and drove it into the hotel yard between stacks of beer kegs waiting to be collected by the brewery. He left his case in the car and made his way back on to the wharf. An isolated, single-storeyed building, little more than a hut, had a faded signboard advertising snacks. It was better than nothing, but he was surprised on opening the door to find a dozen or more customers at plastic-topped tables. Like the men under the verandah, several of them wore blue jerseys and peaked caps. There were a couple of card games in progress with money on the tables and the place had the atmosphere of a club, so that they seemed to look at him with mild hostility. Strangers out of season are as welcome as winter blow-flies.

The man behind the bar looked up from reading his newspaper. He had the features and build of a heavy-weight all-in wrestler, close-cropped black hair almost met his eyebrows over the low forehead, his nose was broad and flattened and he had heavy, stubbly jowls.

He acknowledged Wycliffe curtly, Wycliffe ordered coffee and a ham sandwich.

'Only cheese.'

'All right, cheese.' He waited while the man drew his coffee and slapped two pieces of bread around a piece of rubbery cheese.

'Fifteen pence.'

Wycliffe took his food to an empty table near the bar and the wrestler returned to his paper. Wycliffe watched the card players playing amid a litter of tea cups; the air was pungent with the smoke of strong tobacco. There was little conversation and what there was was fragmentary and allusive; some of it might have referred to the dead woman but he could make little of it. Every now and then someone would break out into a ribald laugh. He was about to order another coffee when the door opened and a man walked up to the counter watched by all of them. He was in his early forties, lean and athletic, with strong features and straight, thin lips. Wycliffe thought that he must have paid more than a hundred guineas for his suit, which was tailored to emphasize his slim waist.

'Has Jewell been in?'

The wrestler was respectful, subservient. 'Not since this morning, Mr Bryce. If he comes in . . .'

'Tell him to get in touch with me at the office.'

The man caught sight of Wycliffe, gave him an appraising look, ran his eyes over the others and walked out, leaving the door open behind him. The men were looking after him and one of them got up and shut the door.

'Bryce? Is he one of the brothers?'

The wrestler folded his arms on the bar counter. 'That was Mr Sidney. As far as the business goes, he *is* the brothers.'

'I thought Matthew was the eldest.'

'He is, but Mr Matt has other interests, Sidney is the second one.'

Wycliffe waited for him to enlarge, but he was disappointed. 'Is the young one in the business?'

'George?' A short, humourless laugh, but no comment. One or two men from the tables were beginning to pay attention to the conversation.

'Boslow – where is it?'

The big man looked him over. 'Are you press?'

'No.'

'Up the river beyond the timber-yard. Follow the waterfront.' He turned away decisively.

After a second cup of coffee Wycliffe walked along the wharf, upstream. A fair, roundabouts, dodgems and a few stalls and booths occupied a broad stretch of tarmac which was probably a car-park at other times. Three or four caravans and a couple of lorries were parked against the high wall which separated the ground from the churchyard and the fair people were hanging out their washing on improvised lines. Wycliffe skirted the fair and reached the ferry slipway. The weird contraption was in mid-stream, making for the western shore; he noticed that the great chains anchored on the slipway were motionless. He picked his way among the dinghies and small power boats drawn up on the wharf by the boatyard and came to the cannery. The cannery looked new: glass and concrete, with a glimpse of white tiles inside. A hiss of steam and a faint smell of fish. Treen Canneries Ltd.

Treen Coal Company was next door. A coaster was being unloaded by grab and telpher, bridging the wharf and dumping the coal directly into the yard. A buffer-stop marked the end (or the beginning) of the railway track.

The sky had cleared at last, baby blue with white cloud masses near the horizon, and the sun was warm. The tide was ebbing strongly. Wycliffe walked on the sleepers like a schoolboy. After the coal-yard, the timber-yard, surrounded by a high fence. Here the family declared itself: Bryce Brothers, Timber and Builders' Merchants. A circular saw screamed tormentedly. Beyond the timber-yard a well-maintained road cut off to his left, presumably returning to the town; the wharf petered out but the railway track continued, running under the trees by the river. On a bend, a quarter of a mile farther upstream, he could see the little station, the terminus for passenger traffic. The trees were part of an estate and a little way along the road Wycliffe could see impressive gate posts and a drive entrance. This must be Boslow.

Matthew Bryce's wife had been found in the river. Matthew had interests which absorbed him to the exclusion of the family business. Sidney was the man to be reckoned with there. And George, the youngest, was rather a sour joke. Wycliffe sighed. Sometimes he baffled himself. Any other detective would have been fully briefed on the family by now. Back in his office, simply by picking up the telephone, he could have learned a great deal from Harker of the Divisional CID. Even more if he had paid a call at the local nick instead of walking in the sunshine. Sometimes it seemed that he had an antipathy for facts.

He left the railway and walked along the road as far as the drive gates. If the place had been a remand home, a school, or a home for unmarried mothers, it would have been better cared for. The gravelled drive was weedy and the laurels and rhododendrons were rampant. All the same, Wycliffe, though a socialist by birth and conviction, felt a pang of regret whenever he heard of an estate falling into the hands of some welfare organization or the municipal park keeper. Tree choppers, all of them! He walked up the drive. It was designed, of course, to make you wonder what you would find around the next bend, and there were several bends before the shrubs ended and he found himself looking across an acre or so of rough grass to a smallish Regency house with bow front and first floor verandah, washed out pink stucco and white woodwork. It reminded him of an iced cake.

Away to his right there was a lake which seemed to be half covered with water plants and beyond that, the fringe of trees by the railway track.

'Are you looking for someone?'

A girl, seventeen or eighteen, slim as a boy and almost as tall as he was. She had her jet black hair gathered into a pony-tail and she wore a faded checked shirt, blue jeans and flip-flop sandals. She must have walked on the grass or he would have heard her.

'Is this Boslow? I'm looking for Mr Bryce.'

'Which one?' She eyed him, it seemed, with suspicion, reluctant to give him information.

'Mr Matthew. Do all three brothers live here?'

She looked vague. 'It's my father you want; you'd better come up to the house.'

'So you are . . . ?'

'Grizelda Bryce.'

She was good-looking; an oval face with high cheek-bones; warm, brown skin, freckled under the eyes. Her lips were surprisingly full and sensuous – the only sensuous thing about her. Her manner struck him as odd, not hostile, but detached; it seemed to him that he was only engaging part of her attention. They started to walk towards the house.

'I'm a detective – Chief Superintendent Wycliffe.'

'You've come about my mother?'

'I'm sorry about what has happened; it must be a terrible shock for you and your father.'

She said nothing. They did not cross the grass but followed the gravelled drive, a concession to elegance in the great sweeping detour which it made.

'They think it wasn't an accident, don't they?'

'That's what we've got to find out – how your mother came to be in the water.'

She looked at him, a sidelong glance. 'She did it herself!' Her manner was almost spiteful.

'What makes you think so?'

She shook her head.

He always felt at a disadvantage when questioning girls, especially respectable ones. His wife, Helen, said that it arose from childhood repression. 'You are still at school?'

'I've just left.' Listless.

'Boarding school?'

'No!' With emphasis.

'How old are you?'

'Eighteen.'

'Are you going to University?'

'That's their idea.'

'Who are they?'

'My mother, my uncle . . .'

'Not your father?'

She shrugged.

'And what about you?'

'I want to finish with it.'

'With what?'

'With studying.'

'To do what?'

Shutters down. 'I don't know.'

'Boy-friend?'

She seemed about to protest but changed her mind. 'No.'

Despite her apparent calmness and reserve she was very unsure of herself. Even physically she had not yet acquired the grace of movement which would come with the confidence of full maturity. Every posture, every step had in it an element of bravado, a trace of aggression.

'You didn't get on very well with your mother?'

'Who told you that?' Anger flared.

'You did.'

'Clever!' She was contemptuous.

They walked in silence for a dozen steps. 'When did you last see her?'

'Haven't they told you?'

'I want you to tell me.'

She stopped walking as though telling her story needed concentration. 'I saw her last Thursday evening – when we had supper. I had a headache and I went to bed early. Next morning my father told me that she had gone to stay with an aunt in St Ives.'

'On the spur of the moment?'

'It happens like that. Aunt Joyce is mother's sister and she's married to Francis Boon, the sculptor. She sometimes threatens to commit suicide and they ring up Mother to come and stay with her. It usually means that she thinks she is pregnant. Francis is a Catholic and she's frightened of having children.'

'How many have they got?'

'They haven't got any.' Her flat tone was a comment in itself.

'And your aunt rang up on Thursday evening?'

She frowned and looked very young. 'That's the funny part about it: she says that she didn't. In any case, Mother didn't go there.'

'But you and your father thought that she had?'

'Yes. It wasn't until yesterday – Monday – that Uncle Sidney rang up to speak to her and found that she wasn't there.'

'Have you any idea where she might have gone?'

'None.'

Wycliffe let it go. They entered the house. The hall was dominated by a staircase of white-painted iron which swept upwards in an opulent curve, but the paint was chipped and the ironwork was dusty. She led him to a door at the back of the hall and into a room with french windows opening on to a cobbled yard. She looked round as though expecting to see her father but the room was empty. 'Wait here; I'll go and fetch him.'

The room had once been the library of the house and there were still a great many books about, but much of the shelving was occupied by mechanical models, models of steam engines, pumps, pit-head gear, hoisting engines and even sections of steam boilers. Every spare bit of wall space was crowded with faded photographs of machinery, foundry operations and mine workings. A large table placed between the windows was littered with prints depicting more machines. The whole place was musty, the books mildewed and the dust was everywhere.

Wycliffe was kept waiting only a couple of minutes before the girl returned with her father. Matthew was a bigger man than his brother with more flesh on him. He looked a good deal older, with sparse, grizzled hair, shaggy eyebrows and a looseness in the skin under his chin. One eye was bleached and glazed, partly covered by a permanently drooping lid, but the other was brown, sparkling and youthful. He evidently cared little for his appearance: his corduroy slacks were too large and almost threadbare and his polo-necked sweater had worn through at the elbows.

'Good of you to come!' A firm handshake. Bryce swept a few books from a chair on to the floor and Wycliffe sat down. 'Drink? . . . No, of course not – too early. Run along, Zel, there's a good girl.' A boisterous assured manner, but the glance of the good eye was restless, flitting everywhere, and there was not a scrap of repose in his whole body. Wycliffe thought that his nervousness was temperamental. Neuroses are supposed to go with the lean, hungry look but in Wycliffe's experience at least as many victims are well covered.

Wycliffe said something soothing and sympathetic and added, 'I understand that you have identified your wife's body, Mr Bryce?'

'The body? Oh, yes, I have been over with Inspector Harker. It's Caroline all right, no doubt about that, poor girl.' His manner was a detached kindliness as though he were speaking of a casual acquaintance, but he looked at Wycliffe anxiously. 'Have you decided that there is something suspicious about her death?' He sat in the swivel chair by his work table.

'The circumstances make an inquiry inevitable, sir.'

'By a detective chief superintendent?' He smiled. 'Or has my brother-in-law been pulling strings?' He raised his hand when Wycliffe would have answered. 'I'll be frank. If my attitude seems strange it's because there was no love lost between Caroline and me. We lived our separate lives and tried to see as little of each other as possible.' As he spoke he pivoted himself back and forth on the swivel-chair but his lively brown eye never left Wycliffe's face.

'Your daughter seems to think that her mother took her own life.'

'Is that what she said?' He stopped fidgeting, evidently surprised. 'I wonder why? There's no knowing what goes on in her head.'

'You don't agree?'

'That Caroline killed herself? Of course I don't, and Zel doesn't believe it either. You couldn't live in this house for a week without realizing that the one person Caroline would never harm would be herself. Zel knows that as well as I do.' He broke off and looked at Wycliffe with the air of one who has been frank at some cost and is rather proud of it.

'Do you think that her death was accidental?'

Bryce placed his hands between his knees and clamped them there as though to restrain their activity. The damaged eye gave him a somewhat lugubrious expression but he seemed sincere enough. 'I find it difficult to imagine Caroline meeting with that kind of accident. A car smash, certainly – she drives like a fiend. But how could one drown in the estuary except when bathing or boating? And I can assure you that Caroline did neither.'

He produced a crumpled packet of cigarettes and after offering them to Wycliffe straightened one and lit it. His lips were an incongruous feature, delicate, thin and sensitive like a girl's, and the filter tip of the cigarette scarcely seemed to touch them. Wycliffe got out his pipe and lit it, puffing out little spurts of grey-blue smoke. 'Why should Zel tell me that she thought her mother had committed suicide if she thought no such thing?'

Bryce pondered. 'Zel is a very intelligent child. She

has probably come to the same conclusion as I but carried her reasoning a step further.'

'What does that mean?'

The cigarette made Bryce cough. 'Zel evidently thinks that her mother was murdered and she's afraid that I did it.'

'She is protective where you are concerned?'

'Very. The poor child, she hasn't had much of a life.'

'You are being very frank.'

Bryce crushed out his half-smoked cigarette. 'I've no option. Plenty of people will tell you of the life Caroline and I led.'

'You saw your wife last on Thursday evening?'

'Yes.'

'When Zel went to bed with a headache?'

He made a small gesture of assent.

Out in the yard fat pigeons were strutting up and down, pecking between the cobbles. The yard was in shadow but the sun caught the lichen-covered roof of the old stables, making the colours glow.

Zel came in. 'You're wanted on the telephone.'

It was Franks, the pathologist, breezy as ever. 'I tried the nick but they hadn't seen you so putting two and two together . . .'

'What have you got?'

'Can I speak freely?'

'As far as I can see there's only this one phone.'

'Good! The woman certainly wasn't drowned: she collected a hefty crack on the base of her skull before she was put into the water. The blow killed her.'

'How long before she was put into the water?'

Franks sighed. 'You know as well as I do that it's impossible to tell with any certainty. At a guess I'd say not less than twenty-four hours; but I could be a hell of a lot wrong.'

'So it must be murder.'

'Seems like it, though I remember one case, not unlike this, where it turned out to be accidental death. A chap painting a bridge fell off, cracked his skull against a projecting bolt, spilling some of his brains, lodged on one of the bridge piers, then slid off into the water at least twenty-four hours later. His mates never missed him, his wife reported to the police when he didn't come home and his body was fished out of the drink three days later. Fortunately he left traces of his passage on the bolt and on the bridge pier.'

'But in this case . . .'

'In this case the skin wasn't broken. A neat job.'

'Not a very powerful blow.'

'No, though I'd say a fairly hefty weapon, something about an inch-and-a-half in diameter, round. A piece of iron or lead pipe would fit the bill.'

'In your opinion, how long has she been dead?'

Franks hedged. 'You know the score. Strictly off the record, I'd say one day before she was put in the water and perhaps three or four days since then.'

'She seems to have gone missing on Thursday evening.'

'That would fit. Incidentally she had a deeply incised post-mortem wound right round her left leg above the ankle.

'A weight tied on?'

'Wired more likely. It must have broken loose.'

'That clinches it then. Even your bloke on the bridge didn't tie a weight round his ankle.'

The telephone was in a little room off the hall and Wycliffe could see most of the hall through the open door. Even so, he lowered his voice. 'You've examined the organs, of course?'

'I haven't had a chance yet. Anything special in mind?'

'Nothing more than the obvious.'

'OK. I suppose I shall be seeing you?'

'Probably.' Wycliffe said 'Goodbye' and rang off.

2

When Wycliffe rejoined Bryce the sun had moved round a little and the yard was filled with sunshine which even reached into the room, emphasizing its dust and shabbiness. Bryce was at his table, sorting papers.

Wycliffe's mood had changed: he was more relaxed, less official, as though he had established a right to be in the house. Instead of sitting down he stood, smoking his pipe and looking at the models and photographs. 'You are interested in the history of engineering?'

'I've been fascinated by machines ever since I was a boy.' Bryce came over and joined him. 'For forty years I've collected models, prints, photographs and every scrap of information I've been able to lay my hands on. I'm talking about real machines – with fly-wheels, cranks, cogs, belts and pulleys – not the newfangled things where you press a button and you hardly know whether the damn thing is going or not!' He was fiddling with his models, taking them off the shelves and putting them back again as though for the sheer pleasure of touching them. 'It's bred in the bone, I suppose. One of my ancestors – another Matthew, with his brother, Tobias, worked with William Murdock for the Boulton and Watt team. Then they broke away and set up a foundry on their own a bit farther up the river from here. They were the original Bryce Brothers. The foundry is gone but the house they built is still there. In 1860 the firm built a new foundry on the site of the present timber-yard and that continued in production without a break until 1919.'

Outside in the sunshine Zel was scattering grain for the pigeons and from time to time she glanced into the room to see what was happening.

'As a matter of fact, I'm writing a book – *Machines of the Industrial Revolution* – written from the stand-point of the practical engineer.' The one good eye seemed to question Wycliffe, seeking his approval. 'I suppose you think this is a futile way to spend one's time?' He waved his hand vaguely to indicate the things around him.

Wycliffe mumbled something non-commital. He moved round examining the models and photographs with Bryce on his heels. On one of the shelves he found a different sort of photograph, a studio portrait of a girl in a tarnished silver frame. He took it down to examine it. The resemblance to Zel was unmistakable. But it was not Zel: this girl had escaped the thick lips and her features were more nearly perfect; her hair, dark and lustrous, fell almost to her shoulders.

'My wife, taken when we were married.'

'She looks very young.'

Bryce took the photograph and studied it brood-ingly. 'She was eighteen, and three months pregnant. I was thirty-seven.' His mouth screwed itself into a grimace. 'If I don't tell you somebody else will. I'm sure that it has become part of the family legend.'

'At what time did your wife leave here on Thursday night?'

'At about ten.'

'She told you that she was going to visit her sister?'

'Yes. She came in here and said that Joyce

had phoned and that they were going to send a car for her.'

'Doesn't she drive herself?'

'I told you, like a madwoman; but at present she is under a two-year disqualification – *was*, I should say.'

'Did she tell you why she was going?'

'There was no need. Joyce is married to the sculptor, Francis Boon. They are both neurotic and they seem to move from one crisis to the next. Caroline acts as a sort of referee . . .'

'And the car came for her at ten?'

'She came in here at about that time and said, "The car is here; I'm going." She was wearing out-door clothes.'

'You didn't see her off?'

'No.'

They moved back to the chairs and Bryce lit another of his crumpled cigarettes.

'Zel had gone to bed when your wife left. Who else was in the house?'

'Only Irene.'

'Irene?'

'My cousin. She acts as housekeeper; in fact, she runs the place with the help of a daily maid.' He brushed ash from his cardigan on to the floor. 'On Thursdays Sidney spends the evening at the Golf Club and he's rarely in before midnight. He's Chairman or President or something.'

'He is unmarried?'

Bryce nodded. 'And likely to stay that way.'

'And what about your youngest brother?'

'George? What's he got to do with it?'

'Doesn't he live here?'

For some reason Bryce seemed to become cautious. 'No, he took a place of his own some years back.'

'What did you and your wife quarrel about on Thursday evening?'

Bryce paused to consider his answer but he did not deny the quarrel. Wycliffe's pipe had gone out and after looking into the nearly empty bowl disconsolately he put it into his pocket.

'It was about business,' Bryce said, 'not a personal thing at all.' He hesitated, then seemed to make up his mind. 'I suppose you'll have to know sooner or later.

'My brother Sidney, Caroline and I are directors of the family business and yesterday, Monday afternoon, we were supposed to meet with representatives of a large West of England firm to sign transfer documents.'

'A merger?'

'A sell-out! Under my father's will our family business was turned into a limited company with my brothers and I holding the shares. As the eldest son I received a controlling interest, but a few years back when we needed more capital for expansion, Caroline offered to put in a substantial sum of money she had received under her father's will. In return she was allocated shares amounting to about one sixth of the paper capital . . .'

'Enough to cost you your control of the company.'

'Exactly; though the fact hardly bothered me at the time. We are a prosperous concern, the profits have always been good and I saw no reason why there should be a difference of opinion on major policy. Neither was there until six months ago when we received an offer to buy us out. Sidney had meantime acquired George's shares and as he might reasonably expect a managing directorship on the new board he was strongly in favour. I was equally strongly against.' He broke off. 'You appreciate the position?'

Wycliffe grunted. 'It's not difficult; the decision rested with your wife.'

'Precisely, and she supported Sidney.'

'Because the offer was a good one or because she was opposing you?'

Bryce shook his head. 'For both reasons, I should think. I suppose that she might have been glad to frustrate me and at the same time, by obtaining cash or a holding in the new company, she would, no doubt, feel freer to go her own way.'

'If your wife had sold out her holding for cash, how much would she have received?'

'Around fifty thousand pounds for an original stake in the company of ten thousand. As I said, the offer was a good one.'

'Yet you opposed its acceptance – why?'

Bryce smiled. 'I suppose because I feel some obligation to a business which has sustained the family for a century and three-quarters and because I believe that a business which is too big for every employee to know the boss is a bad business.' He stopped and shrugged his massive shoulders. 'There are many reasons but they would bore you, I am an anachronism in modern business as Sidney never tires of telling me.'

Did this mild-mannered man realize that he had gone a long way towards making out a case against himself for murder?

'I understand that it was your brother who telephoned and discovered that Mrs Bryce was not with her sister?'

Bryce nodded. 'He rang from the office yesterday morning. He was worried about the meeting in the

33

afternoon and wanted to make sure that Caroline would be there. When he found that she was not with Joyce he telephoned me here. At first I couldn't understand what he was talking about, he was so angry . . .'

'Angry?'

'He thought that I had played some trick on him – that I knew where Caroline was and that I had persuaded her not to come to the meeting.'

'And now?'

'I am afraid that I don't understand . . .'

'What does your brother think now?'

A quick smile. 'You will have to ask him that. Since the meeting yesterday we have scarcely spoken.'

'The deal fell through?'

'I refused to sign the transfer documents, naturally.'

Naturally.

'Were you surprised when you heard that your wife was not with your sister?'

'Of course I was surprised.'

'Worried?'

A curious look which Wycliffe could not interpret. 'I did not suppose that anything very terrible had happened to her.'

'What did you suppose?'

Bryce's manner was calm and grave; indeed he seemed more at ease now than when Wycliffe first arrived. 'I thought it very likely that Caroline had used a visit to her sister as a pretext.'

'For what?'

'Two or three days spent with another man – it wouldn't have been the first time.'

'Your wife was unfaithful to you?'

'Habitually.' The only sign of emotion was a restless movement of the right hand, ruffling the papers on the table.

Long years of police work had failed to inure Wycliffe to this intimate, probing surgery, but it had to be done. 'You know the man?'

Bryce nodded.

'His name?'

Bryce hesitated.

'It will not be difficult to find out.'

'My brother, George.'

'You accepted this situation?'

Bryce drew a hand across his forehead as though ridding himself of an invisible cobweb. 'I regarded it as one of the hazards of marrying a girl twenty years younger.'

'Detective Superintendent Wycliffe stated that the possibility of foul play had not been excluded.' That would be his press release; but it would be enough. Suspected murder of sister of one of Britain's most colourful politicians. They would have a field day. Bellings wouldn't like it. For Wycliffe it would probably mean a complicated, tedious and frustrating inquiry. For all those at all well acquainted with the dead woman it would mean irksome, persistent questions, an intrusion into their privacy, the airing of little vices and the exposure of protective lies. For Wycliffe's team it would mean hundreds of hours of unwanted overtime and reams of paper.

Now was the time to mobilize his team, to choose his operational HQ and get to work; but he was reluctant. He preferred to hang about this house, getting used to the feel of it, getting to know the people who lived in it. He got up, walked to one of the windows and stood staring out into the yard, trying to persuade himself that an hour one way or the other would make no difference.

'Who do you think killed your wife, Mr Bryce?'

Bryce ran his fingers over the ridged corduroy of his trousers, exploring the velvet feel. 'I don't know.'

'Do you and your wife have separate rooms?'

'Yes.'

'I would like to see your wife's room.'

'To see her room? Why yes, of course!' He led the way out into the hall and up the white staircase. In his slippers he had the flat-footed walk of an old man. The carpet on the stairs was dusty and threadbare, dangerous in places. At the top, a long corridor bisected the house lengthwise with rooms opening off on each side. Bryce went to the left and opened a door into one of the front rooms. He stood aside and allowed Wycliffe to go in first.

It was a large room, a sitting-room, and in contrast with what he had seen of the rest of the house, it was modern, uncluttered and scrupulously cared for. It could have been a set for a photograph to illustrate a Habitat catalogue; slatted wood furniture with bright orange cushions, adjustable pendant lamps with lustrous green shades, and shaggy, Scandinavian rugs on a polished, wood floor. There was a large nest of shelves against one wall housing some paper-backed books, a rack of records and a record player, a few pieces of Copenhagen pottery and a transistor radio. Wycliffe wandered round like a dog sniffing out the topography of an unfamiliar backyard. The records seemed to be exclusively 'pop' and the paper-backs included a fair sprinkling of sexy best sellers. All very adolescent.

'Does your daughter use this room?'

'Zel?' He looked surprised. 'No, she has a sort of den in one of the attics.' He added after a moment, 'If you want Caroline's bedroom, it's through there.'

He pointed to a door set back in an alcove by the fireplace.

The bedroom was smaller than the sitting-room. Originally it had probably been a dressing-room but Caroline had made it into a luxurious and very feminine bedroom. Wycliffe sank to his insteps in a shell-pink carpet, the walls were ivory white and there were two geometrical abstracts mounted on plinths on the wall above the bed. The bed itself looked like a pink soufflé. It was double, but it seemed unlikely that it had ever been shared with Bryce. There were built-in floor-to-ceiling cupboards with ivory-white sliding doors and gilt fittings. Wycliffe slid back one of the doors. He knew little about women's clothes but enough to realize that here was what the well-dressed woman wore and plenty of it.

'I suppose you have no idea what clothes your wife took with her?' It was silly to ask; what would Bryce know of his wife's clothes? He was looking round her bedroom as though he had wandered unexpectedly into some rather embarrassing, exotic place.

'I've no idea.' He looked bewildered.

'Only a week-end case.' Zel was standing in the doorway of the bedroom, watching. She had changed into a washed-out blue linen frock and her hair, released from the pony-tail, reached to her shoulders, soft and lustrous like her mother's in the photograph.

'How can you possibly know?'

It was her father's question but she spoke to Wycliffe. 'There's only one case missing. I looked.' She went to the cupboards and slid back one of the doors. There were three white pigskin travelling cases standing in a row and room for a fourth.

'Do you know your mother's clothes well enough to tell me what is missing?'

She was so calm and matter-of-fact that it was difficult to remember that she was the dead woman's daughter. 'She must have had with her a knitted twin-set in a sort of cinnamon colour and a day dress. There's a white mack missing and a long summer coat, light fawn with brown wooden buttons. I expect she was wearing the twin-set and the mack . . .'

'You've checked her clothes?'

She looked him straight in the eyes. 'I wanted to be sure.'

'Of what?'

She shrugged. Then, to her father, 'Aunt Mellie rang up.'

'Mellie? What did she want?'

'She's only just heard about Mother.'

Bryce sighed. 'My sister, Melinda, Mr Wycliffe.'

It was the first Wycliffe had heard of a Bryce sister. 'Isn't she concerned with the firm?'

Bryce shook his head. 'She never got on with Father. In his will he left her a sum of money but she wouldn't accept it. She's married to a seaman and she has a small place up on the hill above East Treen.' He gestured vaguely across the estuary.

He was out of place and uncomfortable in these elegant, feminine surroundings. In any case, he wanted to get back to his engines. 'Do you want me any more, Superintendent?' He hesitated. 'Zel can show you anything you want to see and she can tell you as much as I can . . .' He escaped like a fish let off the hook.

Zel was eyeing Wycliffe appraisingly. 'You think that he doesn't care; but he's very upset.'

'And you?'

'Of course!'

He followed her back into the sitting-room and started to prowl around. It wasn't a systematic search; what he did was what a really inquisitive stranger might like to do to a room which interested him.

'Your mother had a car?' He had found a log-book in her name in one of the drawers of the bureau.

'A Mini. My father doesn't drive much; when he wants to go anywhere he has one of the works cars.'

'Can you drive?'

'No.'

'Where is the Mini now?'

'I don't know; it isn't in the garage.'

In one of the other drawers there were clippings from women's magazines, mainly beauty and health hints, and underneath, a slim book which he lifted out: *The Postures of Love*. (Thirty-five photographic plates. Send £3. Delivered in a plain wrapper.) He caught Zel's look of contempt, slipped the book back and shut the drawer.

'Do you want to see anything else?'

'I don't know – perhaps.'

Caroline Bryce was thirty-four, young enough to make a fresh start, old enough to feel threatened by time. Emotionally immature and chasing after something she wouldn't have recognized had she found it. And she had got herself murdered.

'Who runs the house, pays the bills – that sort of thing?'

'Cousin Irene. She's a sort of housekeeper and she's been here ever since I can remember.'

Getting an eighteen-year-old girl pregnant had probably been Bryce's one great sexual adventure. At thirty-seven. Then, at any rate, he must have known what it was to succumb to passion. But now? And what had happened in the intervening years? Wycliffe had learned long ago that few men live entirely without sex.

'At what time did you go to your room on Thursday evening?'

'About nine, as I told you. I didn't feel well, it was the first day of the curse.'

He was surprised by her bluntness, which seemed out of keeping with her general demeanour. 'Did you go straight to bed?'

'Almost.'

'You didn't hear anything from downstairs? Your mother telephoning, talking, quarrelling – anything?'

'I sleep in one of the attics.'

'Are you keeping something from me, Zel?'

Her soft black hair tended to slip forward, hiding part of her face, and from time to time she would sweep it back in a gesture which had become automatic. 'I don't know what you are talking about.'

'I think you know more than you have told me.'

She moved to one of the windows and stood looking out over the park. 'I saw her go if that's what you want me to say.'

'I want you to tell me the truth.'

'That is the truth, I saw her go from the window of my room.'

'I should like to see your room.'

She turned without a word and went to the door. He followed her into the passage and up narrow stairs, lit only by a murky skylight, to a long corridor carpeted with worn sisal matting. 'Don't think I couldn't have a proper room if I wanted one. I like it up here.' She unlocked and opened a green-painted plank door and stood aside for him to go in.

It was a large attic with a dormer window, furnished as a bed-sitter with odds and ends of furniture which looked as though they had been rescued from a lumber room; but the overall effect was pleasing. A table in front of the window had on it an aquarium, a rectangular tank with glass sides. Graceful, feathery water-weeds kept the water fresh and several small greeny-brown fish swam amongst them. Two or three ram's horn snails scavenged over the glass.

'Are you interested in this sort of thing?'

She gestured vaguely, refusing to be humoured.

There were bookshelves covering most of one wall; school books and paper-backs stuffed in anyhow – a motley collection like the shelves one sees outside junk shops.

He went to the window. The attic was at the back of the house overlooking the cobbled yard and, beyond that, the back land and its junction with the inland road from the town to the station. There was a street lamp on the corner.

'You saw your mother from this window?'

'Yes.'

'At what time?'

'About ten o'clock, perhaps later.'

'Had you been looking out of the window for an hour?'

He saw the faint sneer on her lips. 'I had been to bed but I couldn't get to sleep.'

'So you got out of bed and looked out of the window?' He was trying to needle her into a show of spirit but her face went blank again and she answered flatly.

'I got out of bed to get some aspirin and as I passed the window I saw the light go on in the garage – it's switched on from the kitchen. Then I heard the back door open . . .'

'So you went to the window to see who it was?'

'Yes, and I saw her crossing the yard carrying one of her suitcases.'

'She went to the garage?'

She nodded. 'The one where she keeps the Mini.' She pointed to the second of four garages which had once been stables.

'She drove off in the Mini?'

'Yes.'

'So no-one came to fetch her.'

'No.' She hesitated then added, 'I think she told Father someone was coming to fetch her because she knew he would make a fuss about her driving while she was disqualified.'

'You did not really believe that she had gone to visit her sister?'

'No.'

'What time did your Uncle Sidney come home on Thursday night?'

She looked at him, obviously surprised at the change of subject. 'I don't know, he's usually late on Thursdays because he spends the evening at the Golf Club.'

'Does he have his own rooms?'

'He has a bedroom, of course, and his own sitting-room, but he eats with us.' She was peering down into the aquarium tank as though the conversation had ceased to interest her. She picked up a glass pipette with a rubber bulb at one end and started to fish round the tank as though trying to capture some creature on the bottom.

'What are you doing?'

'I was trying to get this leech.' She allowed water to flow up into the pipette and withdrew it, holding it up for Wycliffe to see the tiny, worm-like creature writhing in the tube. 'They're pests: they attack the other animals.' She squirted the contents of the pipette into a saucer and returned to search the tank for other victims.

Wycliffe was at a loss: it was rare in his professional experience to be treated so casually. 'Seeing your mother go off like that you must have wondered where she was going?'

She was intent on the capture of another leech. 'I could guess.'

'What?'

'That she was going to a man.'

'But you didn't contradict the story which your father told you next morning – that she was staying with her sister?'

She emptied another pipette-full into the saucer. 'I got two that time!' She looked up at him with candid brown eyes. 'No, I didn't contradict him; there didn't seem to be much point.'

While she continued to poke about in her tank Wycliffe took stock of the room. Part of one wall was occupied by a large and faded poster about hippie flower power, mildly erotic; there were several pop star pin-ups and two framed pencil portraits, one of Zel and the other of a youth with serious eyes and sensitive features. They impressed him by their economy of line and a haunting delicacy almost impossible to describe.

'These are good!'

She looked over without much interest. 'They were done by a girl at school.'

'An odd sort of girl.'

'What?' He had more of her interest now. 'Why do you say that?'

'This portrait of a young man is certainly a self-portrait.'

'Clever you!'

'Boy-friend?'

'You could call him that.'

'A secret?'

'It was until she found out.'

'Your mother? What did she have to say about it?'

'You really want to know?'

'I asked.'

'She said, "Do you let him screw you? If you do you'd better go on the pill: I don't propose to have a squalling brat about the place!" Now I've shocked you, I suppose.'

'No, but was that your intention?'

She had her back to him, bent over the tank and she did now answer.

'Who is he?'

'That's my business.'

Wycliffe did not argue. 'Well, I must go; but I shall be back with more questions. If your father wants me he can telephone the local police station.'

'All right, I'll tell him. Can you find your own way down?'

He went down the attic stairs to the first floor landing. The house was utterly silent. Not even the ticking of a clock. He went along the broad corridor, passed the top of the stairs and opened a door at random. A bedroom, furnished with heavy mahogany pieces, a thick red and black carpet on the floor. The bed was a massive affair with scroll-work and bunches of fruit at the head and foot; it was covered with a real old patchwork quilt. The room reminded Wycliffe of his grandmother's bedroom and it had probably been the same when the Bryce parents slept there. For some reason which he could not explain to himself he knew that it was Sidney and not Matthew who slept there now.

A door off the bedroom opened into a small bathroom which looked like an exhibit from the showrooms of some specialist in sanitary ware. Of course, that would be part of the family business. Over the wash-basin a mirror-fronted cupboard contained a variety of toilet preparations, aftershave lotions, hair creams, hand creams, talcum powders and a few patent medicines.

The great double wardrobe in the bedroom held several suits, all of good quality, and there was a bow-fronted chest of drawers filled with shirts and underclothes, expensive and beautifully laundered. Sidney was a dandy.

Next door was the sitting-room, another large room, with leather armchairs, a mahogany desk with silver ink-stand and pen-tray and massive, glass-fronted bookcases with books on economics, company law, accounting and business management. It was less a sitting-room than an office but, again, Wycliffe had the impression of a stage set rather than a room where somebody lived and worked. It was a strange household; not, perhaps, a household at all – just a house in which people lived, each, it seemed, with a feverish desire to impress his or her personality on part of it. Matthew in the old library, Caroline in her aggressively modern suite, Sidney with his ponderous Edwardian elegance. And Zel – did she live in a real world?

He went over to the bookcases. A dull lot. Below the glass-fronted cases were cupboards and Wycliffe opened the doors. These cupboards too, were full of books which were more interesting. Romances by the score. As far as he could tell they seemed to be mainly stories of chivalry, the sort of thing most boys grow out of in their teens: fair damsels in dark towers rescued by fearless, spotless and apparently, castrated Sir Galahads. But at the end of one of the rows he found a nest of books which were quite different: *Girlhood, The Psychology of Female Adolescence, The Difficult Years, You are Sixteen* and *Sex and the Young Girl*. All were fairly new. They were objective, factual works with nothing pornographic about them; but strange reading, all the same, for a bachelor of forty-five. He shut the doors. When you lift a stone you never know what you will find underneath.

He let himself out into the corridor, closing the door silently behind him, and reached the top of the stairs in time to witness a little scene in the hall below. Bryce was there with a woman, a dumpy little grey-haired woman in her fifties, dressed for out-of-doors and carrying a loaded shopping bag. Her free hand rested on his arm and she was looking up at him with an expression of concern. Bryce stood, his back to Wycliffe, shoulders drooping, trousers sagging. The woman saw Wycliffe almost at once and drew away. Wycliffe went down to be introduced.

'Superintendent! I thought you'd gone. This is my cousin, Irene – Miss Bates. She keeps house for us. She's just come back from shopping.' He added, 'I'm afraid she's a little deaf.'

At first she reminded Wycliffe of the little painted figure of the farmer's wife which used to be included with toy boxes of farm animals. She was comfortably plump and motherly with rosy patches of colour on her cheeks; all she needed was a white apron to tie round her waist. But looking more closely he could see the moist eyes, the loose, wet lips; and the colour of her cheeks began to look more like an alcoholic flush than a sign of health.

'This is a dreadful business!' Her voice had that

curious tone quality which comes after years of partial deafness.

'Just for the record, Miss Bates, where were you when Mrs Bryce left the house last Thursday evening?'

She looked at him blankly.

'You'll have to speak up,' Bryce said. 'She won't wear a hearing-aid. The superintendent wants to know where you were on Thursday evening when Caroline went out.'

Wycliffe was at a disadvantage. He wanted to ask cousin Irene a few questions – but not standing in the hall with Bryce acting as interpreter. 'Is there somewhere . . . ?'

'Take the superintendent up to your room.' She seemed reluctant, but Bryce held out his hand for the shopping bag: 'I'll drop that in the kitchen.'

'No!' She twitched the bag away from him and both men heard the clink of bottles.

Her sitting-room was on the first floor overlooking the yard. It was a comfortable-looking room, but shabby and in need of a good clean. It had an old-maid smell compounded, amongst other things, of stored linen, camphor balls and cats. A giant, doctored tabby slept in a saggy, chintz-covered armchair; he opened his green eyes momentarily, stretched, unsheathing his claws, then went back to sleep. There was an old-fashioned treadle sewing machine in the window and a television set by the fireplace. A second door opened into an adjoining bedroom and Wycliffe could see part of the foot of a brass bed and the corner of a white quilt.

'Were you here on Thursday evening, Miss Bates?'

She looked at him vaguely. 'I'll just go and take off my things.' She disappeared into the bedroom, taking her shopping bag with her. He could hear her moving about and, after a moment or two, the sound of something being poured into a glass. She was fortifying herself and, indeed, when she came back into the room a few minutes later she seemed more alert and her eyes had lost their moist, glazed look.

'The evening Mrs Bryce left . . .' Wycliffe reminded her.

She sat on the arm of the cat's chair. 'I'm here every evening from about nine o'clock after I've cleared away the supper things.'

'Do you remember last Thursday evening in particular?'

She stroked the cat's sleek body absent-mindedly but her eyes avoided Wycliffe's. 'I suppose it was just like any other evening.' Her glance fell on the machine in the window. 'I remember; I was sewing.'

'Did you look out of the window?' He had to repeat the question.

A decisive shake of the head. 'No, what would I look out of the window for?' She seemed to be following her own train of thought and Wycliffe's questions were an intrusion on it; yet she was frightened of him. Every now and then he would catch her stealing sly, wary glances but she never met his eyes directly. 'There's nothing to see out there, only the yard. In any case I was sewing.'

'So you didn't see Mr Bryce or Mrs Bryce?'

'No.'

'Or Zel?'

'I didn't see anyone!'

'And you didn't hear . . . ?' He broke off and apologized. 'Was there nothing that struck you as unusual that evening?'

'Nothing.'

'Were you surprised to learn next day that Mrs Bryce had gone to stay with her sister?'

She dabbed her lips with her handkerchief. 'Why should I be? She often went there.'

'Have you any idea who might have wanted to kill her?'

'No.' Then she added, 'Nobody in this house.'

'How can you be sure?'

She shrugged. 'I live here.'

'What about Zel?'

For once her eyes met his, anxious and scared. 'What do you mean by that?'

'What sort of girl is she?'

Her plump, ringed fingers were intertwined and she was alternately tightening and relaxing their grip. 'Like most young girls these days, I suppose.'

'What does that mean?'

'Hard and selfish – spoiled.'

'Not by her mother?'

She gave him a quick, knowing look. 'You're right there! Her mother understood her too well. Her father and her Uncle Sidney made up for it though.'

He got out his pipe and asked permission to smoke. She watched him fill and light it. 'My brother always smoked a pipe; I like to see a man with a pipe . . .' The tension relaxed.

'This seems an odd sort of household. How long have you been here?'

'Since I was . . . about fifteen years.'

'You came after Zel was born, then?'

'She was three. I'd been keeping house for my brother; he died of a coronary and as they needed somebody here Matt asked me to come. I've been here ever since.'

'How do you get on with the brothers?'

She took time to consider. 'Matt is kindness itself, gentle as a lamb . . .' She put her hand to her mouth and did her best to suppress a belch. 'George was wild but, speak as you find, he was all right with me.'

'And Sidney?'

She pursed her lips.

'You don't like him?'

'I like a man to be a man; he's more like a woman.'

'He seems very fond of his niece.'

'Too fond if you ask me!'

'What about Caroline Bryce? How did you get on with her?'

She pondered. 'I didn't approve of her way of life, of course, or of the way she treated Matt, but outside of that I had no complaints.'

'Friendly?'

She looked at him briefly. 'She used to come and talk with me sometimes. Now and then she would come up here of an evening after supper and we'd have a good old gossip. She was lonely – like me.' Cousin Irene looked bleakly from her TV set to her sewing machine.

'What sort of woman was she?'

'Not so bad as she was painted. She ought never to have married Matt and she knew it. She needed affection but Matt was incapable of giving it to her. And Zel . . .'

'What about Zel?'

'In my opinion she wasn't a natural daughter. Caroline used to say they'd poisoned the child's mind against her, but if you ask me that one never had much love for anybody but herself.' She sighed breathily. 'I shall miss Caroline.'

Wycliffe wondered if the two women had exchanged

their confidences over a glass or two of gin. 'Somebody murdered her.'

She looked at him sharply. 'Why do you say it like that ?'

'Because it's true and it's my job to find out who did it. It's your duty to help me but I think you're holding something back.'

He spoke kindly but her agitation returned. She got up and went over to the window, ostensibly to straighten the curtains. 'You've no right to say that ! I've told you everything I know !' She turned to face him and he was astonished at the change in her: the colour had spread to the roots of her hair and she was flushed as though of a fever. He looked round the pathetic, spinsterish room and wondered what possible good he was doing by upsetting her.

'Don't upset yourself.'

'That's all very fine; you come here badgering me then you tell me I'm telling lies ! You've no right to accuse me . . .'

Wycliffe stood up. 'I'm not accusing you of anything, Miss Bates. Thank you for being helpful.'

'You're going?' She watched him, tense, on the verge of tears.

He nodded. She crossed the room to stand beside him, looking up in what seemed to be an agony of apprehension. 'You won't . . . ?'

'I won't what ?'

She shook her head. 'Nothing. Take no notice, I'm not well. Anybody will tell you I'm not well.'

He opened the door, certain that before it closed behind him she would be at the bottle.

At the bottom of the stairs he met Bryce. 'You're wanted on the telephone.'

He went into the little room off the hall.

'Wycliffe.'

'Mr Bellings for you, sir. Hold on, please.'

An interval, a click, then Bellings' voice. 'Is that you, Charles? . . . I've been trying to get you for the past hour! . . . I spoke to the local sergeant but he didn't even know you were in the town! In any case, I thought you were going to stay at the Manor Park?'

'Have you been ringing them too?' It was the first time Wycliffe had spoken.

'I didn't have to. Clement Morley did so then telephoned me when he couldn't locate you.' The PRO in Bellings was outraged. Crime left him unmoved unless it made an unsightly kink in his graphs, but anyone who made a balls-up of public relations was for the hot seat. 'I gather that there is some doubt?'

'About what?' As usual, Wycliffe's response to the stimulus of his immediate superior was a retreat into sullen taciturnity.

Bellings was reluctant to be more explicit. 'About the cause of death.'

'There's no doubt about that; she was murdered.' He was tempted to add, 'Unless she fell off a bridge backwards, hit her head in falling, landed on a buttress then slid off into the water two or three days later . . .' But Bellings was without humour.

'I see.' A moment of silence. 'The Chief is very concerned about this case, Charles . . . Do try to be a bit accommodating where Morley is concerned – it oils the wheels . . . Are you there?'

Wycliffe grunted.

'I hope that I have made the position clear?'

'As crystal!'

'The Chief . . .'

Wycliffe dropped the receiver, his lips moving in silent imprecation. He got out his pipe and lit it again before leaving the house.

3

The estuary looked even more attractive, calm and peaceful in the sunshine. Three dinghies, two with white sails and one with blue were weaving complex patterns between the mooring buoys off the town, and a tug, towing a mud-barge, pushed swiftly downstream for the open sea, raising a herring-bone pattern of swell which rocked the smaller craft. As he drew near the timber-yard a long drawn-out wail announced the end of the working day and by the time he reached the gates men were streaming out, some on bicycles, some on foot. Half-past five.

Wycliffe's acquaintance with Clement Morley dated back more than thirty years to when they had been schoolboys together. Morley's father, a tool-setter by trade, had started a small engineering works in 1939 and it had grown with the war and the post-war boom until, in the early sixties, the old man had sold out to one of the big boys for over a million. Young Clement had shown a taste for politics and after a year or two in local government, learning the trade, he put up for parliament. He had been an MP since 1954 and in 1959 he served for a few months in a junior ministerial post. He was noted for his speeches, delivered with almost Churchillian fire and eloquence, on any subject linked with his particular brand of morality, from bare bosoms on TV to full frontal nudity on the stage. A prime minister had once referred to him as 'Our Champion of the non-event', but Morley had a strong non-confirmist lobby behind him.

Before collecting his car from the yard Wycliffe went into the hotel and made a telephone call from the public box. As a result of the call several people had to change their plans for the evening. In particular, Chief Inspector Gill, Wycliffe's No. 2. The recent lull had made it possible for him and his wife to lead a more normal home life, and for this particular evening they had engaged a baby-sitter so that they could go out together and sample the swinging night life of the city. (Two tickets for the University Theatre followed by a nosh-up at the Chinese.) Instead, Gill would be travelling to Treen with three others of the squad, a detective sergeant and two constables, one a woman.

Detective Inspector Harker of Divisional CID who had taken Bryce to identify his wife's body, would be drawn back into the case with his sergeant and three constables from the uniformed branch. Finally, a police driver with a truck was detailed to tow one of the mobile HQ caravans to Treen to provide a base for Wycliffe and his team.

Having thrown these several stones into the private pools of other people's lives, he felt that he had made a start on the case. Soon it would begin to move out of his control, seeming to take on a life of its own.

He asked one of the hotel staff where Clement Morley lived.

'Up the hill out of the town; you can't miss it – there's two great gateposts with greyhounds on the top . . . On the right about a mile and a half out . . .'

He found the posts and followed a short drive which brought him on to a gravelled sweep in front of the house where a black Mercedes was parked. It was a terrace from which the ground fell away rapidly in grassy slopes ending in woodland. The slopes were so steep that he could see the distant blue of the sea above the trees. The house was squarely built of grey stone without a creeper to relieve its barrack-like severity. He parked his Zephyr by the Mercedes and rang the doorbell. A formidable female with a disturbing squint admitted him. 'I'll see,' she said.

Wycliffe was received by the ex-minister in his office, where he sat at a table littered with papers. A red-head, wearing a tight, black jumper suit hovered at his elbow and was dismissed with a nod as Wycliffe came in.

Morley was the same age as Wycliffe – forty-five – but his hair, which had been jet black, was now grey. He had been a tall, weedy youth and he was still thin and bony except for a well-developed paunch. He still wore large, circular spectacles which gave him an owl-like expression and made his features seem even leaner and more angular in contrast with his thick, protuberant lips. Those lips had fascinated and repelled Wycliffe as a boy and they did so still, their moist, pink fleshiness reminded him of entrails.

'Wycliffe? Wycliffe? That's an uncommon name. I went to school with a Wycliffe.' He was boisterously patronizing. 'You wouldn't be Charlie Wycliffe? – Charlie Wycliffe – that's it! Well, well!' He laughed. 'After all these years!'

Wycliffe refused a cigarette and listened to the ex-minister reminisce about their school days, memories so different from Wycliffe's own that he found it difficult to believe in their common origin. At any rate, the great man seemed little grieved by his sister's death.

'Half-sister. Caroline was my half-sister, you must remember . . .'

Wycliffe had forgotten that old man Morley had married twice; his first wife had died while Clement was a young child.

'Now, tell me about poor Caroline.' He took a cigarette from the box on the table, fitted it into a holder and made a ritual of lighting it. 'Did she take her own life?'

'She was murdered.' Wycliffe was blunt but Morley seemed unaffected. He nodded as though the news was no surprise.

'I see!' He made himself more comfortable in his upholstered swivel-chair. 'We've not been particularly close in recent years . . . To be frank, her conduct had been something of an embarrassment to me. All the same . . .' He looked at Wycliffe through a thin haze of cigarette smoke. 'I would be the last one to want anything hushed up – you quite understand, Wycliffe?' He gestured with his large, bony hands which had black hairs on the backs. 'You've no idea who did it?'

'Not yet.'

He shook his head. 'It all comes of marrying a man old enough to be her father and a fool at that! I warned her at the time but it was never any use talking to Caroline. Obstinate!' He chuckled briefly. 'She got that much from the Morleys anyway. My colleagues on the front bench . . . But that's another story.' He was silent for a while. 'At the same time I hope that you will be discreet. I sent for you to tell you how important it is to avoid unnecessary scandal, scandal which could do me and the party a great deal of harm and nobody any good . . .'

Wycliffe looked at him blandly. Morley was sitting

with his back to the window and through the window Wycliffe could see the tops of the trees and the sea beyond. He was watching a ship creep almost imperceptibly along the distant horizon and remembering a visit he had once paid to the Morley home while they still lived in a council house. A leggy little girl of three or four had insisted on showing him her dolls; that little girl must have been Caroline. Another little girl, much younger, sat on her potty in the middle of the room to the intense embarrassment of Clement who kept trying to stand between her and Wycliffe.

Morley was beginning to look at him uneasily for he had scarcely spoken since coming into the room. Now he began to ask questions.

'Is this your permanent home, sir?'

'I come here whenever I can get away from London.'

'When did you arrive here last?'

'On Wednesday.'

'Any particular reason for this visit?'

Morley looked annoyed. 'I scarcely think . . .'

Wycliffe's expression was utterly blank but his eyes worried Morley.

'There was not too much on and I felt in need of a break. I get in a round or two of golf . . .'

'You are Chairman of the Building Trades Corporation?'

Morley was eyeing the chief superintendent with concern. 'I suppose Bryce told you?'

'About the take-over – yes.'

'That was the reason for my visit; it is a deal I have planned for some time.'

'I understand that Sidney Bryce was in favour of the sale?'

'Of course he was! He's a businessman and he

knows on which side his bread is buttered. We've been friendly for years – even Caroline married into the family.'

'But Matthew opposed it?'

Clement Morley blew through his thick lips. 'Matt, as I said, is a fool! He lives in the past, and that, as my old father used to say, never filled anybody's belly!'

'Surely Bryce Brothers must be small beer to a firm like BTC?'

The coarse hands dissented. 'By no means! They have a large turnover and though they have fingers in too many pies, a programme of rationalization would . . .'

'And it all depended on your half-sister?'

'What?' Morley seemed, suddenly, nervous. 'I don't understand you.'

'Which way she voted.'

For some reason he was relieved. 'Oh, yes, that is quite true; it all depended on Caroline.'

'And she wanted the deal to go through?'

His manner was edgy. 'Certainly! She had very good reason – a handsome profit on her investment.'

'Matthew would have stood to gain more than his wife, yet he was opposed to the sale.'

Morley laughed. 'Matthew is a sentimentalist but there is . . . was no sentiment in Caroline where business was concerned.'

'When did you last see her?'

'Caroline? We saw little of each other. She made a good deal of unpleasantness when my father died and, in any case, her way of life was repugnant to me.'

'To your knowledge, did she have any enemies?'

'Enemies?'

'She was murdered; somebody must have killed her.'

Morley stubbed out his cigarette in a crystal ashtray. 'A woman in her position, living as she did . . .'

'What was her position?'

It was clear that Morley resented having his words challenged in this way. 'Surely it is obvious! A woman with a fair amount of money in her own right and with wealthy and influential connections . . .'

Wycliffe realized that Morley was anxious for him to place a certain interpretation on his half-sister's murder but he was by no means sure that he understood the reason for this anxiety. To proclaim to the world that she had been murdered by her lover would surely do no good to the Morley image?

Morley shuffled the papers on his desk and went through the ritual of positioning his blotter and pen-tray. 'Have you any knowledge of Caroline's private affairs? Her will, her business papers – that sort of thing?'

'Not yet.'

'I take it that you will . . .' He broke off.

'That I shall what?'

Morley was embarrassed. 'Go through her effects.'

'Certainly.' Wycliffe was cool. He wished that he could smoke but he did not want to establish the kind of relationship which would make it possible. He remained silent while the grandfather clock by the fireplace checked off the seconds with a heavy tick. Morley seemed to be absorbed in his private thoughts. Wycliffe looked round the gloomy, depressing room with its modern oak panelling, its heavy furnishings; a ponderous and pompous room like its owner. Over the mantelpiece were two photographs in ornate gilt frames, photographs which Wycliffe vaguely remembered from the Morley living-room of thirty years ago. The Morley parents. The old man – by no means old when the photograph was taken – a factory worker in his Sunday suit, butterfly collar, waistcoat and watch chain. A compelling face, thin-lipped and resolute. Morley's mother, a girl in her twenties, a flapper with crimped, bobbed hair, a bold face and thick, protuberant lips which she had handed on to her son.

'You did not get on well with your step-mother, did you?' The question, in its offensive irrelevance, arose from a sudden memory of the hard-faced blonde who had taken the first wife's place and dominated the little council house. He recalled vividly her manner of speaking to young Clement, the barbed words, uttered with barely concealed antagonism.

Morley was obviously put out but he answered with fairly good grace. 'She resented me as the child of the first marriage.'

'Is she still alive?'

'She died a year before my father.'

For a little while Morley seemed to have forgotten the deference due to him; now he remembered. 'Well, Wycliffe, if that is all, I'm a very busy man.' He stood up. 'I think we understand each other. I merely wanted to make it clear that, while I have nothing to hide, I should not enjoy having the family's linen washed in public.' He nodded in dismissal but Wycliffe sat tight.

'I have one or two more questions.'

The ex-minister had already begun to sort through his papers and looked up in surprise. 'Indeed?' He glanced at the clock. 'I can give you another five minutes – what is it you wanted to know?'

'Some information about George Bryce.'

The thaw was immediate. 'George?'

'I gather that Matthew and he did not get on.'

Morley smiled. 'That is an understatement. Matt ordered him out of the house two years ago.'

'Not because he had sold his share in the business ?'

Morley lit another cigarette and exhaled slowly. 'That may have had something to do with it but there was more.'

'Your half-sister?'

Morley growled something unintelligible.

'What sort of chap is he?'

'George? A rake and a wastrel with the years catching up on him.'

'Where does he live now?'

Morley jerked a thumb over his shoulder. 'A small place by the river, above the station. Actually it's the house the original Bryce brothers built for themselves – Foundry House, they call it.'

'Alone?'

Morley frowned. 'His is the only name on the voters' list.'

Wycliffe stood up.

'Is that all?'

'How does he make a living?'

Morley sneered. 'By his wits.'

'Was he never in the business?'

'No; when he left school he went, of all things, to study medicine. Even more surprising, he qualified . . .'

'So he's a doctor?'

'A doctor without patients. After he had completed his hospital training he decided that medicine was not for him – too much like work, I imagine. To the best of my knowledge he's never done a day's work since.'

It was clear that, at last, Wycliffe had given him the

chance to say what he had been waiting to say all along.

'Well, thank you for your help, sir.'

Morley came with him to the door and saw him to his car. 'About George, you may be on to something. I've heard queer stories . . .'

Wycliffe drove back to his hotel and ate an indifferent meal, scarcely noticing the food. Only three tables were occupied, grouped round an electric heater; the rest had chairs stacked on top of them. A party of commercial travellers ate at one of the tables and at another a middle-aged couple in country tweeds looked like survivors from an era when people took walking holidays. The Swedish girl, whom the commercials called Nora, waited at table. When Wycliffe baulked at a selection of tinned fruits swimming in custard she seemed to be so affronted that he ate them to avoid a scene.

Afterwards he went in search of the police station.

The late summer evening dusk filled the narrow streets of the little town with purple shadows. There was no-one about; even in the square only a black mongrel dog, making a tour of the perimeter, sniffing at the corners and cocking his leg. The fair was in full cry, and the racing canned music and the amplified bleat of some pop singer hung like a pall over the houses. Wycliffe found the police station in a little cobbled court off the square, a small granite building with a blue lamp and the date 1896 over the door.

In the office a little old lady, crisp and neat as a Meissen figure, was laying down the law to the sergeant behind the desk. 'I have no wish to cause unpleasantness, Sergeant, but one cannot stand by while children are permitted, perhaps encouraged, to commit theft.'

The sergeant's eyes were glazed in patient

resignation but when he caught sight of Wycliffe he became brisk. 'We will certainly look into your complaint, Miss Allard, and thank you for reporting the incident.'

But the old lady had not yet made her point to her entire satisfaction. 'I am not one to interfere, but I ask you, Sergeant, what would young Billy be doing with a travelling case? It was a quality article and by no means worn, though a little mud-stained.'

'Exactly, Miss Allard; I have noted your description.'

'I mean, his mother has had plenty of time to report the find if she had any intention of doing so. Billy had it with him when he came from school . . .'

Her voice, a gentle sawing sound, like wind in the rushes, monotonous and soporific, seemed as though it might go on for ever but in the end the sergeant edged her to the door and eventually through it.

'I'm sorry about that, sir!' Then he added, 'I've been expecting you, sir. Mr Bellings telephoned.' A gentle, well-merited rebuke, for, whatever one's rank, it is unforgivable to prowl about on someone else's patch without a word.

'You know why I'm here?'

'Yes, sir.'

Wycliffe well remembered the day when the top brass used to ask him damn silly questions like that – but you have to say something.

'Do you know much about the Bryces?'

Penrose hesitated. 'A little, sir. Everybody speaks well of Mr Matthew though why, I'm not quite sure. He's hardly ever in the town and they never see him in the yards. All the same, the idea seems to have got round that he keeps Mr Sidney in check – stops him turning the time and motion boys in – that sort of thing. Sidney runs the business and he's got a bit of a reputation as a would-be slave-driver, out for every penny.'

'What about George?'

The sergeant frowned. 'He's nothing to do with the business as far as I know.'

'What's he like as a man?'

'He's got a temper: more than once he's come near to being in trouble with us when he's had a few drinks too many . . .'

'Women?'

'It seems so. They say he was kicked out of the house by his brother for having an affair with his sister-in-law. That was before my time, but I do know her car is parked on the waste ground by Foundry House often enough.'

'Has Sidney got any vices?'

'Not unless making money and playing golf are vices.' The sergeant smiled. 'He doesn't seem to have time for anything else.'

Wycliffe was staring out of the office window which was frosted halfway up. Just across the court, in a little sitting-room, three children were watching television, their intent faces lit by flickering light on the screen. He got out his pipe.

'What was that about a travelling case when I came in?'

The sergeant was young and anxious to make a good impression. 'One of our problem families, sir, the Jordans. Father is on the Assistance for nine months of the year, there are six kids, three under school age, and mother puts the older ones up to nick anything they can lay their hands on. Proper female Fagin she is, if you understand me, sir.'

'I have read *Oliver Twist*.'

'Of course, sir. Well, this old lady, Miss Allard, lives next door with her two sisters and they are always complaining about what goes on in the Jordans'.'

'What are you going to do about the travelling case ?'

'I'll get one of my chaps to call in the morning.'

'Go there yourself – now. I'll look after the shop.'

'Sir ?' He had been warned about Wycliffe's eccentricities.

'I'm interested in that case. Try and get hold of it before they've flogged whatever was in it.'

The sergeant put on his helmet and left. Wycliffe was alone in the little office. Light green paint peeling off the walls, the slightly greasy pitch-pine of the counter and the fly-blown face of the clock on the wall. Twenty years ago he had spent a few months as a sergeant in a little office almost the twin of this. He sat on the stool and put his elbows on the counter, smoking his pipe and wondering what he would do if he had a customer.

But, as always, he found it impossible to think logically, constructively. He supposed that there were people who could sit down and consider any problem which faced them, weigh the evidence and decide on a course of action. There must be such people, otherwise there would be no mathematicians, no philosophers, no scientists; but from a very early stage in his career he had realized that he was not one of them. At first he had worried about this defect, sometimes he still did, but the fact remained that whenever he decided to 'think things out' his mind became vague, filled with hazy pictures, half-remembered phrases, and with anxious reflections on his own conduct. Was he making a fool of himself?

That was the question which constantly cut across any serious attempt at analytical thought.

The atmosphere of Boslow lingered with him, an old and beautiful house which should have left some impression of grace and elegance, however decayed. Instead it had depressed him. His dominant recollection was one of near squalor and tattiness despite the incongruous and rather tasteless luxury of Caroline's room and the heavy ostentation of Sidney's. The house was a shell, like a hermit crab's, not made for the life within it.

Fugitive images flitted through his mind. Matthew Bryce, nervous, intense and, somehow, not quite genuine. Wycliffe found it hard to put his finger on it, but he had the impression that Bryce had been playing a part. There were moments when he had caught that restless, intelligent eye upon him as though he were gauging an effect. Then there was Zel, curt, grave, with an air of matured sadness which seemed to have little to do with her mother's death. 'She did it herself!' had been Zel's first reaction. Then she told of seeing her mother leaving with a suitcase, driving off. And he could hear Bryce's voice, speaking of Caroline's inopportune pregnancy: 'I am sure that it must have become part of the family legend.' Had he said it with a sneer? For all his Robert Owen socialism he seemed to have a certain arrogance. And lastly, the pompous Morley, falling over himself to involve George. 'I've heard some queer stories . . .'

He got off the stool to stretch his legs and stood by the window. Across the court the sitting-room was in darkness: the children must have gone to bed or, perhaps, to the fair. He became aware again of the music which must have been a background to his thoughts all the time; it filtered through into the secluded court, muffled by the houses.

Jimmy Gill arrived with his detectives before the sergeant returned. Gill was young for a chief inspector, rugged and tough. While strangers were invariably surprised to learn that Wycliffe was a policeman, Gill would never raise any eyebrows on that score. Wycliffe liked him and the two men got on, largely because their temperaments were complementary.

He came into the little office, blinking in the light, for it was now quite dark outside.

'Where are the others?'

'Waiting in the car.'

'You'd better book them in at the hotel on the quay. That's where I am and there's plenty of room.'

Gill lit one of his little black cheroots which he smoked instead of cigarettes, hoping that they were less hazardous. 'The van will be here soon, I passed it about twenty miles back. Where shall we put it?'

Wycliffe had in mind a little patch of grass between the ferry slipway and the boatyard. He told himself that it was conveniently placed between Boslow and the town, but this was rationalization: he fancied that particular spot for his command post.

'I've been in touch with the electricity people and the telephone engineers. They will be here first thing.' Gill never forgot anything. The caravan had electric lighting run off batteries but the batteries had to be charged from the mains.

Wycliffe gave him a potted version of the case to date and when Sergeant Penrose returned with the travelling case his office was full of tobacco smoke. Chief Inspector Gill was perched on a stool like a gargoyle on its plinth and Chief Superintendent

Wycliffe was sitting on the counter with his legs swinging.

'What's all this then?' Gill slid off the stool and took the case. 'Let's see what's in it.'

'It's locked, sir; they hadn't got round to opening it.'

Gill took a paper clip from the counter, straightened it, then put a small hook on one end. With this he attacked the locks on the case and in thirty seconds he was able to snap back both catches. He looked round for approval – it was his party piece – but Wycliffe was staring out of the window and the sergeant was too intimidated to say anything. Gill started to lift out the contents of the case, dropping the items one by one on the counter. Wycliffe turned to watch. The fawn coat with the wooden buttons was there, so was the dress; a spare set of underclothes, a nightgown, a bed-jacket, quilted dressing gown, toilet articles, a pair of mules, three paper-backed thrillers and a packet of indigestion tablets.

Gill said, 'Not my idea of the gear for a dirty week-end.' He picked up his half-smoked cheroot from the counter, where it was beginning to scorch the varnish. 'Where the hell was she going with that lot?'

Wycliffe turned to the sergeant. 'Where does the boy say he got the case?'

'He found it under Gummow's Bridge, sir. There's a stream . . .' He showed them on a wall map of the district. Gummow's Bridge carried the station road over a small stream which, later, ran through Boslow and emptied into the lake. It was not more than two hundred yards from the back door of Boslow.

It seemed incredible that the dead woman had carefully packed her case then thrown it into a stream

69

two hundred yards from her home. But almost as incredible that she had been attacked within a few seconds of leaving the house. Even if she had been, why had her attacker been in such a hurry to throw out her belongings? It didn't make sense.

'You'd better see about getting your people booked in, Jimmy; then you can send them to fix up the van.'

The newcomers, divisional and area, disturbed the off-season peace of the Treen Hotel, but the proprietor, a youngish man with a magnificent growth of red moustache and sideboards, entered into the spirit of the thing, so that when Gill came up to the superintendent's room at a little after ten, every man and the policewoman had a bed to go to.

Wycliffe had the french window open and was standing on the balcony, leaning on the rail, smoking his pipe. The room was in darkness. 'There's a bottle of beer on the dressing table.'

'Thanks, but I had a couple with the landlord before coming up,' Gill said and joined Wycliffe outside.

The evening was mild and the waters of the estuary faithfully reflected every mast-head light and every street lamp on the wharf. Across the water Treen's other half looked remote and secretive with its pattern of lights and unaccountable patches of darkness.

'It doesn't make sense, Jimmy. She leaves home at around ten on Thursday evening. The girl, Zel, saw her go with her suitcase, and heard the car drive off. Two hundred yards away the suitcase is found under a bridge. I suppose she could have picked up somebody just outside the house . . .'

Gill was following his own thoughts. 'She must have had a handbag; we must search the stream tomorrow.'

'We've got to find the car.'

They smoked in silence for a while. Wycliffe was

the first to speak. 'The things in her case . . . does anything strike you about them?'

'Except that they seem a pretty unglamorous collection, no.'

'Has your wife ever been in hospital?'

'Hospital? But the Bryce woman was due back for the take-over meeting on the Monday. In any case, ten o'clock at night is no time to be going into hospital unless you're an accident case or an emergency.'

'The night train for London leaves the junction at 10.45; the junction is seven miles away.'

'Are you suggesting that she was off to some plush pad in London for an abortion?'

'Franks wouldn't have missed that.'

'What then? I don't get it.'

'She could have been ill, or thought she was.'

'A couple of days under observation in some clinic – is that it?'

'It's possible. We must ask Franks to take a second look; the indigestion tablets may be a lead.'

Gill whistled. 'I'll get on to the railway; she would have booked a sleeper . . .'

'I have and she did.'

'Her doctor would know.'

'We shall have to find out who he was.'

'No time like the present!'

Wycliffe sighed. 'Sleep on it, Jimmy!'

All the same, for a long time after Gill had gone the chief superintendent remained on the verandah, arms resting on the wooden rail, smoking his pipe.

Caroline Bryce had been murdered when she was setting out for London. Whether the hospital idea was right or wrong remained to be seen, but who had reason to kill her? Obviously Matthew Bryce – a double motive: her conduct as a wife and the fact that she would destroy the family business by which he set such store. If Bryce had killed her the fact that she intended to be away for a few days would give him a breathing space before people started to ask questions. But how to explain the travelling case? Only a fool would pitch the thing in a stream near the house unless it was intended to be found. And what about the car? Presumably it had been used to transport the body to a suitable spot from where it could be dumped in the river; but where was the car now? And if Zel was telling the truth her mother had left the house alive and alone.

His pipe had gone out and it was getting chilly. A damp mist was creeping up the estuary from the sea so that navigation lights now shone dimly and there was scarcely anything to be seen of the lights of East Treen. Wycliffe knocked out his pipe and returned to his room, closing the french window behind him.

As he was dozing off a phrase recurred to his memory with such clarity that, for a moment, he almost believed that the words had been spoken aloud. 'Nigger lips!' It was one of the unflattering epithets the boys had applied to Morley when he was at school. Wide awake, he fell to thinking about Morley's lips, those incongruous features which had come down to him from his mother. But why lose sleep over Morley's lips?

4

'Control to all mobiles: Keep look out for red Mini-Cooper saloon, Z, Bravo, Victor, One Five Nine, Johnny . . .'

House to house inquiries, Treen and district: 'Were you in the vicinity of Boslow House on Thursday evening?

'Have you seen a Mini-Cooper saloon, registration number ZBV 159J?

'Were you anywhere along the river bank above the town?

'Did you see anything unusual or suspicious?'

And so on. And so on.

The routine had begun. Already a uniformed constable was hammering away at a typewriter in the HQ room of the caravan while the smell of the night man's bacon and egg still lingered. Two plain-clothes constables were questioning the fair people, having to rouse them from their beds, for they were not early risers.

Wycliffe's office in the caravan was at one end, its window overlooking the estuary. It was small, but convenient. There was a sofa-seat which converted to a bunk, a desk-table, a few built-in drawers, a telephone and a couple of folding chairs for visitors. His visitor now was Jimmy Gill. Gill sat astride his chair, enveloping it, his arms resting on the back, his chin on his arms. He was ugly, with thick, rubbery skin set in deep lines and he had a chronic five o'clock shadow,

73

but Wycliffe had heard that women found him irre-sistible.

'Franks says she'd been in the water three or four days before they fished her out and that there must have been a considerable interval between her death and the dumping of the body.'

'He only gives that as an opinion,' Wycliffe growled. He was never very enthusiastic about Jimmy Gill's excursions into speculation. At this stage it was enough to think about the people involved, to recall what they had said and done and their manner of saying or doing it. But Jimmy was not easily put off.

'When Franks gives an opinion it's good enough for me. So, if she was killed on Thursday night, the body was probably kept somewhere until Friday night . . .'

'Why?'

Gill shrugged. 'Probably because the murderer hadn't made up his mind what to do with it.'

'I don't believe that this crime was unpremeditated.'

'Whether it was or wasn't the body didn't go into the water right away and it's unlikely that anybody would try to do such a disposal job in broad daylight. Even at night the quays and wharfs are well lit.' He massaged the bristles on his chin. 'I've been having a natter with the harbour-master; I'd say she was ditched upstream, beyond the wharf. But in that case it would have to be done within an hour either side of high water, otherwise the body would have to be humped over deep mud.' He consulted his notes. He had arrived only the night before and, presumably, he had slept; but he was fully briefed. 'High water on Friday night was at 21.49 and sunset was at 19.16 so it's my guess that the body was put in the water between ten and eleven on Friday night . . .'

Wycliffe was unappreciative. 'I know how your

mind works, Jimmy, but what we need at the moment is some nice, tangible evidence.'

'A red Mini, for instance.'

'That might help, certainly.'

As though to oblige them both, there was a tap on the door and the duty constable came in looking nervous. 'Message from Information Room, sir – about the red Mini . . .'

The car had been found in a disused quarry on the hill behind the town. Although there was a good enough track running in at the level of the quarry floor, somebody had driven the car over rough ground higher up and pitched it over the brink, to fall fifty feet on to a heap of discarded steel drums, old beds and rusty car bodies.

Wycliffe stood up.

'Are you going there, sir?'

'No, you are, my lad.'

When Gill had left, Wycliffe telephoned the pathologist.

'It's possible that she was due to go into hospital for a period of observation . . .

'I suppose there is no possibility that she was pregnant ? . . . No, just as I thought. Thanks. It could be the digestive tract, perhaps the stomach . . .'

He had decided to call on George Bryce and he set out alone, on foot. He followed the wharf upstream; MV *Alacrity* had finished discharging her coal and was waiting for the tide to put to sea. It was a fine day, blue overhead and cloudless, with nothing to disturb the stillness but the hum of machinery from the timber-yard. He reached the end of the wharf and the entrance to Boslow but he continued along the railway track which ran its course between the estate and the river. There was no proper boundary wall;

only a bank under the elms, covered with moss and ferns, which must have been a paradise of primroses in the spring. On the river side the embankment sloped gently to a narrow beach of muddy shingle which would be covered at high water. It was here that, according to Gill, Caroline Bryce's body had been pushed into the water on Friday night. It would not have been difficult at high water.

He had to step off the track at one point while a diesel engine pulling a few trucks trundled down the line. A quarter of a mile on he came to the station, a single platform with a loop line, a signal box and no-one to be seen. Beyond the station the railway cut across the neck of a promontory which jutted out into the river. It was on this land, about two acres, that the Bryces had built their first foundry and their home – Foundry House. There was no sign of the foundry, but the house, four-square and built of brown stone, rose out of the wilderness of bracken and gorse. A few tall pine trees, stripped of all but their topmost branches, were grouped behind the house. The gorse was in its second flowering, filling the air with scent, and the bees were busy collecting their bonus offer. There seemed to be no direct way to the house, but a broad, muddy track fringed the river and Wycliffe followed it. He came to a stone-built boathouse and a blue Triumph parked in the cleared area round it. There were planks missing from the doors of the boathouse and through the gaps he could see the dull gleam of the water in the dock, but no boat. On the platform beside the dock there was room for a couple of cars so George Bryce probably used it as a garage.

In front of the boathouse some attempt had been made to counter the mud by putting down rubble, and a narrow path led off through the gorse in the direction of the house. He followed the path. There was no sound but the droning of the bees. This seemed to him a place after his own heart; the sunshine, the silence, the neglect and the general air of mouldering decay appealed to a streak of indolence in his nature about which he always felt guilty. He knew that his retirement, when it came, would be as crowded with activity as his working life, and for this, unreasonably, he blamed his wife, for whenever he mentioned his lotus-land dream she said, 'It wouldn't last twenty-four hours!'

In front of the house there was a small area of rough grass and on a rug on the grass a red-headed girl was sunbathing in the nude. She sat up without embarrassment. He noticed that her freckles came down in a deep V between her breasts. She reached for a house-coat and slipped it on. He had the impression that he had seen her before somewhere.

'What do you want?'

'I'm looking for Mr Bryce – Mr George Bryce.'

'He's gone out.' Her manner was remote, disinterested, reminding Wycliffe to the distinguishing characteristic of the modern young, lack of curiosity.

'I'm Detective Chief Superintendent Wycliffe.'

'I know. You came to see my boss, Clement Morley.'

So that was it. Perhaps he was being unfair, but he found it difficult to imagine this girl being much use to a politician except, perhaps, in bed.

'I only work for him when he's down here – just his letters and any typing he wants done.'

'You live in Treen?'

'At the Golf Club – my father is the "pro". I'm Margaret Haynes.' She stood up, scratching her thigh unselfconsciously. 'George will be back soon; you'd

77

better come in.' She picked up her sun-tan lotion and pulled on a pair of sandals. She was pretty but her features were a trifle pinched. Her mouth, in particular, had a mean look.

The sitting-room where she took him was high-ceilinged, with a dusty, plaster cornice and a monstrous ceiling-rose made ridiculous by a dangling electric flex and a bulb without any shade at the end. The furniture was 1930 vintage, imitation leather armchairs with sprung velvet cushions. A carpet-square, threadbare and dusty, made an oasis in a desert of stained floorboards. There was a pervasive smell of dust and damp.

'I'd better put something on.' She left him but returned in a few minutes wearing a sleeveless summer dress. 'Smoke?' She took a packet of cigarettes from the mantelpiece and offered it to him.

'No thanks; pipe.'

'Don't mind me.' She lit a cigarette.

'You do Mr Bryce's letters?'

She frowned. 'I don't think he has any. We're just friends.'

'I believe that Mrs Bryce – Mrs Matthew Bryce was also a friend of his.'

She looked at him coolly. 'He's a friendly man.'

'I suppose you know that she was murdered?'

'Mr Morley told me.' She flicked ash vaguely in the direction of the fireplace. 'Hard luck. But I don't know why you come after George: there's been nothing doing in that quarter for months.'

'They quarrelled?'

'I don't think so; he moved on.'

There were footsteps in the hall, then a voice, 'Maggie!'

She went to the door. 'You've got a visitor, a

78

detective—' She turned to Wycliffe. 'What did you say your name was?'

George Bryce was thirty-four, trying to look ten years younger and almost succeeding; only the lines from his nostrils to his mouth betrayed him. He wore a dark-blue blazer and cavalry twill trousers. His jet black hair rippled back in tight rows of curls. Perhaps the Bryces came of Jewish stock?

'I'm investigating the death of your sister-in-law, Mr Bryce. You will understand that it is necessary for me to know as much as possible about her way of life; about her friends, and about her enemies. You may rely on me not to put a false construction on anything you may tell me; but it must be the truth.' Smooth talk. The dentist says, 'It won't hurt.'

Bryce sat on the arm of one of the leather chairs while the girl lit a cigarette and handed it to him. 'You'd better go.' His manner was brusque.

She looked at him, startled. 'Go? But . . .'

'Just go!'

She was like a little dog who had been kicked. She went as far as the door, then turned back, trying to retrieve something of her dignity. 'I'll see you to-morrow?'

'Perhaps.' Bryce had no thoughts for the girl. It was obvious that his concern was with Wycliffe. 'Well?'

'You were on friendly terms with your sister-in-law?'

'Yes.'

'Intimate terms?'

Bryce made an impatient movement. 'As though you didn't know!'

'Right up to her death?'

Bryce hesitated. 'No.'

'When did your relationship with her come to an

79

end?' Sometimes Wycliffe listened to himself using the euphemistic jargon of his trade and squirmed.

'A couple of months ago.'

'Why?'

'I had been trying to break it off for some time.'

'Why?'

He did not answer.

'Was it because you had found someone younger?'

Bryce fingered his dark sideboards, brushing the soft, tiny ringlets the wrong way. 'No, Caroline was changing; she was becoming . . .' He hesitated for a word.

'Possessive?'

'Yes.'

'Women are apt to when they feel their youth slipping away.'

'I suppose so.'

'Where were you on Thursday night, Mr Bryce?'

'On Thursday? Was that when . . . ?'

'She was murdered on Thursday night, but, according to our expert, her body was not put into the water until later, probably twenty-four hours later.'

'Who's your expert – Franks?'

'Yes.'

'A good man. If he says that, ten chances to one he's right; but it's very odd.' He paused, seemingly engaged in some private calculations. 'I was here on Thursday night.'

'Alone?'

Was there a moment of hesitation? 'Yes.'

'Were you at home all the evening?'

'No, I . . .'

'What time did you return?'

Bryce fingered his sideboards. 'Latish; about half-one, I should think.'

Wycliffe brought out his notebook, which rarely saw the light of day. 'Who were you with?'

Bryce looked at the notebook and frowned. 'I don't want to involve . . .'

'It's your own involvement you need to worry about, Mr Bryce!'

'Very well. We made up a party, three chaps and three girls . . .'

'Names and addresses?'

'Nick Scoble, Paynter's Lane, Bodrifty . . . Alfred Miller, 15 St Clement's Terrace, Treen . . .'

'That will do for the moment. Was Miss Haynes one of the girls?'

'No.'

'When you returned here on Thursday night or Friday morning, was there anyone here waiting for you?'

'No, definitely not.'

Wycliffe was reflecting that at any time Bryce decided to go back to medical practice he would not be short of women patients.

'When did you last see your sister-in-law, Mr Bryce?'

His cigarette had burned down without him noticing and he discarded the stub with a little yelp of pain. 'On Tuesday.'

'Two days before she was murdered?'

'I suppose it must have been. She came here.' He seemed to make the admission reluctantly but Wycliffe was by no means sure that he was not playing a part, rather cleverly. He had placed himself between the Chief Superintendent and the window so that it was difficult to see his face clearly.

'I understood you to say that you had broken with her two months ago.'

'Yes, but she came here and took me by surprise; she wanted to consult me about something.'

'About what?'

'About her health – you know that I'm a doctor?'

'Was Mrs Bryce your patient?'

He shook his head. 'I don't take patients; but she wanted my advice about something which had been worrying her. She had been subject to more or less chronic indigestion and colonic pains.'

'Had she been to her own doctor?'

'She didn't have one. Like a good many women who worry about their health she had a horror of doctors.'

'She was worried?'

'Very.'

'With reason?'

Bryce became cagey. 'I doubt if she had reason for serious concern, though it's difficult to be sure without proper tests. I think the indigestion remedies she took made her colonic condition worse rather than better.'

'You advised her?'

'She refused to go to any of the local men, so I suggested that she booked in at a private clinic for a couple of days so that she could have the necessary tests.'

'She agreed?'

'She asked me to suggest somewhere and I told her of a place in town run by a chap who was at University with me . . .'

'This clinic . . .'

'The Harcourt Clinic, Cherrington Street – it's off Wimpole Street.'

'Did you make the arrangements for her?'

'There and then, by phone. She was booked in

Friday to Sunday. She said she had to be back here for the meeting on Monday.'

'About the sale of the firm to BCT?'

'That's what she told me.'

'Had you heard of the proposed sale before that?'

He shook his head. 'It was nothing to do with me. I sold out years ago, more's the pity. She seemed to think she was on to a good thing.'

Facing the window, as he was, Wycliffe had a clear view of the area in front of the house and he had not seen Margaret Haynes leave. He felt pretty sure that she was listening at the door but it was of no concern to him.

'You and Mrs Bryce parted on good terms?'

'The best. She said that she was very grateful and she seemed to mean it.'

'Although you are a doctor, you do not practise. You live on your investments?'

Bryce lit another cigarette. 'You must be joking! You haven't been talking to the family without discovering that I'm broke. It's no secret; I've been that way for some time.'

'Did you receive money from your sister-in-law?'

'You know damn well I did. You must have found my IOUs – unless . . .'

'Unless what?'

'Unless she'd scrapped them.'

'Why should she?'

'As she was leaving on Tuesday after I'd fixed up the clinic for her, she said, "Thanks, Georgie. I might decide to do you a good turn; I'll think about it." I wondered then whether she meant that she . . .'

'Who do you think killed your sister-in-law, Mr Bryce?'

He frowned. 'I don't know; I can't imagine who would want to.'

'Her husband seems to have had motive.'

'Matt? You can't be serious! Matt wouldn't kill a mouse.'

Wycliffe changed the subject again. 'Your affair with Mrs Bryce seems to have lasted longer than most.'

'I suppose it did; we suited one another.'

'If your brother had divorced her would you have married?'

He seemed amused at the idea. 'You've got it all wrong. Caroline wouldn't have married me if I'd asked her. She wanted security.'

'And you? What did you want?'

He smoked for a while before answering. 'Freedom, I suppose. I still do.'

'Apart from Mrs Bryce, does anyone else from Boslow visit you here?'

He shook his head. 'Only Zel.'

'Zel?'

'She's a funny kid; she used to hang around here quite a bit at one time.'

'But not now?'

Bryce smiled. 'She still comes now and then; she turns up and slopes off as the mood takes her.'

'She doesn't hold your relationship with her mother against you?'

'If she does it's never stopped her coming here.'

Wycliffe seemed to be running out of questions; the silences became longer. 'How did you get on with your father?'

'Father? The old man was all right as long as you did what he wanted. As he had the purse strings, we mostly did – except Mellie. She wouldn't knuckle under to him.'

'I suppose you have somebody in to do the house-work?' Wycliffe had not the least idea why he asked some of the questions, except that they helped him to build up a picture in his mind, to fit people into a context. Zoologists are told that it is unprofitable to study an animal divorced from its environment; Wycliffe thought that the same principle applied to suspects and witnesses.

Bryce was getting impatient with the constant changes of ground and he answered curtly. 'A woman comes in three days a week.'

'Which days?'

'Tuesdays, Fridays and Sundays. On Sundays she's supposed to cook me an evening meal but as I'm usually out, God knows what she does.'

Wycliffe stood up and prepared to leave. As he did so he saw Margaret Haynes run lightly across the grass and disappear along the path through the gorse. He lingered until he heard the car engine start. Bryce heard it too and looked startled but said nothing.

Bryce saw him to the door. 'I would run you back to town but I've rather a lot on at the moment . . .'

Wycliffe said that he would enjoy the walk along the river bank. As he was about to enter the path through the gorse he looked back, but Bryce had already gone inside. The house looked blind and empty, the windows, which seemed to have no curtains, were dark and unreflecting.

The blue Triumph was gone but an old MG sports, looking rakish and sly, was parked nearby. It evidently belonged to George. Wycliffe slid back the bolt of the wicket in the boathouse door and passed inside. He paused to allow his eyes to become accustomed to the dim light, for there were doors on the river side also, though there was a large gap below them to allow for the rise and fall of the tide. The building of the boathouse must have been a substantial undertaking for a channel had been scooped out and lined with stone to give access to the river at all states of the tide. At least, that had been the intention; but long since silt had built up in the dock almost to the level of the mud outside.

The platform beside the dock was paved with stone but it had accumulated a layer of mud which clearly showed the marks of tyres. Wycliffe thought he could make out at least two sets. This was not surprising: evidently he used the place as a garage, and no doubt his visitors did too. He continued to prowl round but found nothing in the least suspicious. When he was about to give up he heard footsteps outside. A car door slammed and the engine spluttered into life. It seemed that George Bryce had given him just enough time to get clear before leaving himself.

He walked back the way he had come. The sun shone brilliantly out of a cloudless sky; red flowers of campion and white umbels of cow-parsnip seemed to wait, still and breathless in the heat. It was more like a day in July except that the leaves would have been a fresher green. He took off his coat and carried it over his arm. Somewhere across the water a clock struck twelve.

After more than twenty years as a policeman Wycliffe was rarely surprised by human behaviour but often puzzled and always intrigued. Matthew Bryce had married a girl young enough to be his daughter; he had turned his back on the business he seemed to love to devote himself to a nostalgic quest for something which was dead and gone. His brother George tried desperately to cling to youth, in order, so it seemed, to live out its sexual fantasies. Then there was the girl, Margaret Haynes. What did she want? Surely not the practised and blunted passions of a man like George? Presumably these people like most others wanted to be happy; consciously or unconsciously they sought after happiness, but what an extraordinary way to go about it!

Sententious thoughts of a middle-aged policeman walking in the sun. 'They grab!' he muttered. But to give him his due, he recognized in them his own humanity and that was what made him a good policeman.

As always he found it easier and pleasanter to reflect on the people he had met rather than to think analytically about the crime. It was obviously possible that George Bryce had killed his sister-in-law. A discarded mistress.

When he arrived back at the caravan he found Jimmy Gill dictating his report to a woman PC. The uniformed duty constable was still hammering away at his typewriter and an alarming quantity of typescript had accumulated in the wire tray at his side. Jimmy followed Wycliffe into his tiny private office.

'Did you get the car?'

'A breakdown truck is taking it to Division. Forensic can look at it in their garage.' Gill perched himself on the edge of the table and lit a cheroot. 'Incidentally I got hold of that kid who found the case – bent from the cradle, that lad – poor little bastard! That yarn about finding the case in the river was all balls. He found it in the car in the quarry but he wanted to keep that quiet so that he could go back and nick what else he fancied. That toffee-nosed sergeant wants his arse kicked . . .'

There was an elemental crudity about the chief

inspector which sometimes irritated Wycliffe. 'Get off my table!'

Gill got off, grinning, and sat on the chair.

Wycliffe had come to a decision. 'I want the boat-house at Foundry House searched. Try not to scare George Bryce if you can help it, but I want the place gone over . . .'

'. . . with a fine-toothed comb.'

'Don't be infantile, Jimmy! And check on these characters; George says he was with them on Thursday night and early on Friday morning. If it's an alibi, see if it stands up.' He handed Gill his notebook with the addresses of George Bryce's friends.

'You think he needs an alibi?'

'I don't think anything; I just want information. Which reminds me, send Birkett to chat up the woman who does for George. She goes there on Tuesdays, Fridays and Sundays so she could have been there when Caroline Bryce visited on the Tuesday. See if you can find out how long she stopped and whether the old girl knows what it was all about.'

Gill stood up and picked a few memorandum slips from the tray on the table. 'There were several calls for you . . .'

'Clement Morley, Bellings and who else?'

'Sidney Bryce wants to know when it would be convenient, et cetera, et cetera . . . and the same from Mrs Joyce Boon.'

'Joyce Boon? Who the devil is she?'

'Wife of Francis Boon, sister of the deceased. They've come up from St Ives and they're staying at Boslow. Apparently they wanted to use Caroline's rooms and she was more than a mite peeved when our chaps told her they couldn't.'

There were two detectives at Boslow, searching

Caroline's rooms and going through her papers with the Bryce lawyer.

Jimmy Gill stopped on his way out. 'There's one more thing – you'll see it in the reports. Our chaps have done the rounds of the fair people and they've turned up a chap called Brandt. His father was a German POW who married an English girl and got himself naturalized after the war. Brandt is a sort of general factotum and hanger-on at the fair.'

'What about him?'

'He's got form. Two convictions for GBH – once on a woman.'

'Don't be daft, Jimmy!'

Gill shrugged. 'You're the boss!'

Wycliffe lunched at the hotel where he was conscious of the surreptitious attention of three divisional men lunching at another table. He could never get used to the fact that most men who worked with him were scared of him, that he had a reputation. When he went into the bar for a drink after lunch they were there before him. He acknowledged them curtly. One, a detective constable with a face and figure like Harry Secombe, plucked up courage. 'Have one with us, sir.'

Wycliffe's bland, expressionless stare almost froze the poor man. 'Thank you – no.'

His response was reflex. If he had given himself time to think he would probably have acted otherwise; but it was always the same. He did not know why. Bellings would have accepted the drink and stood a round or two. 'At least I don't patronize them!' he growled to himself. But why could he never unbend? Was it because he was never sure of himself?

In the afternoon he drove out to Boslow, parked in the drive and rang the bell. The door stood open but nobody answered his ring so he went in. The hall was dim after the bright sunshine outside. Somebody opened a door at the back of the hall and he heard a woman's voice, harsh and discordant. 'You ruined my sister's life and now you've killed her! A young girl she was when you married her, and you, old enough to be her father!'

There was an interjection which he could not hear but it served to inflame her even more. 'You dare to say such a thing! You . . . !' Words failed her and she slammed the door.

Wycliffe had moved towards the scene and now saw that it had taken place in the doorway of Bryce's room. As she turned from the door she saw him and seemed annoyed rather than startled. 'Who are you?'

She had straight, black hair, but very short, and her long face with high cheekbones gave her a masculine look. She was not very tall, thin and bony, and the flowered dress she was wearing hung from her shoulders in ample folds.

Wycliffe introduced himself and she became affable at once. Her recent anger had left no trace; she was neither flushed nor, apparently, ruffled. 'I'm Joyce Boon, Caroline's sister.'

Presumably the little girl he remembered sitting on her potty in the middle of the Morleys' living-room. He sighed inwardly, 'Thirty years!' She led the way across the hall to a room which Wycliffe had not been in before, a large and once elegant drawing-room. Now, however, the furniture was shrouded in dirty and torn loose covers, the carpet was dusty and almost worn through and the faded wallpaper showed great patches of damp around the chimney.

A little wisp of a man with a few straggling blond hairs on his chin was in the act of pouring himself a whisky. He was excessively pale – etiolated, like a plant grown in darkness. 'My husband, the sculptor.' It seemed that he could hardly have the strength to sculpt in anything more refractory than balsa wood.

Boon looked at him nervously, then at the drink in his hand. Wycliffe shook his head.

'Francis has been ill; he's convalescing.' Everything Joyce Boon said seemed to be spoken in capitals.

'Do sit down.' She looked at one of the easy chairs critically before sitting down herself. 'This place! One would think that the Bryces were paupers! I wanted to move into Caroline's rooms but your men would not allow it.' She raised her hands in an extravagant gesture to forestall an apology which Wycliffe had no intention of making. 'You don't have to apologize! My dear man, I'm not a fool! I realize that poor Caroline was murdered and that you have to investigate her death.' She stared at him with great gravity. 'I only hope that you are not too late.'

'Too late?'

She seemed surprised by his obtuseness. 'Don't you think it's very likely that you are? – too late to find any evidence, I mean. After all, Caroline died on Thursday evening and he had three days to cover his tracks. He's been very clever.' She added, having realized a possible explanation of his slowness, 'You realize that Matthew killed her, I suppose?'

Wycliffe was icily cold. 'Perhaps you and your husband will help me by answering some questions.' Without waiting for a reply he went on, 'Mr Bryce says that his wife told him she received a phone call from you on Thursday evening, asking her to come and stay with you.'

'It's a lie!'

'Possibly, but have there been occasions when such a thing did happen? Did you sometimes telephone your sister asking her to visit you at short notice?'

'Sometimes; I'm very highly-strung and Francis is an artist . . .' She spread her hands. 'We have our crises.'

'Is it possible that Mrs Bryce might have used such visits as an excuse to absent herself from the house for other reasons?'

Joyce looked at him wide eyed. 'My dear man! You don't have to mince words with me! Caroline had a man and she used to spend the odd day or two with him when her husband thought she was with me. Why not?'

'Why not, indeed?'

'Her husband could give her nothing – *nothing*. You understand? But she never did it without warning me – in case he phoned.'

Francis Boon had poured himself another whisky and was staring moodily into his glass.

'Did she never consider divorce?'

'Why should she?'

Wycliffe felt like Alice after an encounter with the White Queen. Joyce Boon's attention was temporarily distracted: she was staring at an unfaded patch of wall-paper above the fireplace. 'There used to be a Fragonard hanging there – What happened to it?'

'I've no idea.'

'You remember the Fragonard, Francis?'

Boon only shook his head vaguely.

'It was the only decent picture in the house. I suppose the fool has sold it or given it away . . . Anyway, coming back to Caroline, she *had* to lie to Matthew. I never lie to Francis because he understands me and if I want an affair all I have to do is say so and he understands – completely! It's the only possible basis for marriage.' She looked at her husband. 'As for Francis, if I were a possessive woman . . .'

Wycliffe happened to glance out of the window and saw Zel saunter past. He was reminded of a phrase of Lawrence Durrell's – something about 'the sulking bodies of the young'. Joyce Boon had seen her too.

'And there's Zel – absolutely and completely spoiled by her father and her uncle. She should have been sent away to school, and that was what Caroline wanted, but no, she didn't want to go away from home !' She shook with irritation. 'And they've brought her up to hate her own mother ! Somebody will have to take that girl in hand.'

Wycliffe was feeling the bowl of his pipe in his pocket and reflecting that there must be some profoundly depressing psychological reason for the fact that it gave him satisfaction. 'There are just two more questions, Mrs Boon. First, about your sister's estate: do you know anything of a will ?'

She looked at him in surprise. 'Hasn't the lawyer told you ?'

'I'm asking you.'

She shrugged. 'Well, that's it, isn't it ? Years ago they made wills leaving everything to each other. Recently Caroline said that she intended to alter hers but she never did.'

'Would you have known ?'

'Caroline told me everything; we had no secrets. In any case, if she had changed her will he would have had no reason to kill her.'

'But Mr Bryce is a rich man; the money could mean little to him.'

'Not the money, but his precious company. He's got his majority holding back, hasn't he ?' She sat back in her chair with evident satisfaction. 'You said that there were two things. What was the other?'

'Who was her lover?'

'Why, George Bryce, of course. God knows why. You would have thought one of the family was enough . . .'

'There was no-one else?'

She was emphatic. 'No, there was no-one else.'

'You would have known?'

'I would have known.'

'She was a bitch!' It was Boon's first and only remark.

Joyce looked at him with a tolerant eye. 'Francis never liked her.'

Wycliffe sat staring out of the window. Joyce Boon pursed her lips and waited for him to speak.

'Did you know that your sister was ill?'

'Ill? Caroline was never ill. She never had a day's illness in her life.'

'On Thursday evening when she left here she was on her way to a London clinic for observation . . .'

'I don't believe it. She would have told me!'

Wycliffe said nothing.

'What was wrong with her?' She stood up and almost stamped her feet. 'My dear man! I've a right to know; I'm her sister!'

'She suffered from chronic indigestion and she was afraid that it might be something more serious . . .'

She looked at him suspiciously. 'Are you trying to tell me that she committed suicide? If so, I don't believe . . .'

'No, your sister was murdered.'

As he left the room he almost fell over Irene Bates in the passage. Impossible to believe that she had been eavesdropping so he assumed that she must be waiting to speak to him. 'You wanted to see me?'

She stared at him like a frightened child and her lower lip trembled as though with some sort of tic.

'Did you know that Caroline was ill?'

She looked less frightened. 'She worried about herself: she was terrified of cancer and every ache and pain . . .'

'When she left here on Thursday she was due to catch the night train to London where she was booked in at a clinic for observation.'

The news touched her and she dabbed her eyes with a screwed-up handkerchief. 'Poor girl!'

'I'm going to her rooms to talk to the lawyer; if you have something you want to tell me . . .'

She recoiled. 'I've told you! There's nothing!' She shuffled off towards the kitchen.

Inspector Wills had made a name for himself and a job as a specialist in accountancy, wills and probate. He had assisted Wycliffe before. Lean, dark and precise, he looked more like a company secretary than a policeman. He introduced Wycliffe to the Bryce lawyer, Mr Lambert, middle-aged, plump, bald and jovial.

'You acted for Mr Bryce and his wife?'

'And Sidney.' Lambert grinned. 'When relations became strained between Matthew and his wife I suggested to her that she might find somebody else but she laughed and said it was worth something to have a foot in both camps. Actually we got on very well, poor woman!'

'Anything to tell me?'

'Not much, sir. Mr Lambert is being very co-operative.'

'No point in being anything else, is there?' Lambert

reminded Wycliffe of one of Dickens' more amiable and ebullient lawyers. 'If you chaps don't get what you want one way you get it another.'

'Mrs Bryce's will leaves everything to her husband; it is dated fifteen years ago and Mr Lambert says there has been talk of changing it.'

'Only talk – nothing definite.'

Inspector Wills passed him a sheet covered with figures.

'This could mean something. According to her bank statements these sums have been paid into her account over a period of five years by quarterly instalments. It seems that she had this income of nearly two thousand five hundred a year apart from the return on her investment in the company and apart from what Bryce allowed her.'

'Unknown to me,' Lambert put in. 'Of course I can find out from the bank the source of the payments and I'll let you know unless . . .'

'Unless what?'

'Unless the information is prejudicial to the interests of one or other of my clients.' Lambert seemed to think this a great joke.

'No IOUs amongst her papers?'

'None that we've found.'

5

It occurred to Wycliffe that he was putting off meeting Sidney Bryce. He had an antipathy to businessmen, by which he meant people who put a price tag on everything and judge every issue in terms of economics. He had met businessmen who were not in the least like that but he insisted on regarding them as exceptions to a general rule. In any case he had already seen Sidney Bryce at the snack bar on the wharf and, if looks were anything to go by, he must be the type-specimen of the genus.

He told the duty constable to telephone Bryce Brothers and find out when Sidney would be in his office.

'Mr Bryce will be in his office until six o'clock and he will be expecting the chief superintendent.'

A clearer conscience. His puritan ancestry and upbringing prevented him from ever being entirely at peace with himself unless he was planning or doing something which he found disagreeable. Fortunately women are fundamentally amoral and thanks to his wife, Helen, he was learning to live with an uneasy conscience.

The clock on the shelf above his little table showed half-past three. It was hot. He wrestled with the mysterious mechanism of the caravan window and got it open. A faint, tangy breeze filled the room and rustled the papers on his table. The ferry was on its way over to the east side, carrying a bus and a couple of private cars. He must cross over sometime and explore the narrow streets which ran between the grey huddle of houses round the quay. He picked up a bundle of reports from his tray.

The name Brandt caught his eye. 'Frederick Brandt, 26. Fairground labourer . . . shares a caravan with Margery Cook, 19. On being questioned Brandt admitted that he had served two terms of imprisonment for causing GBH.' A lot more, totally irrelevant, then: 'Brandt stated that he left the caravan, alone, at seven o'clock and returned at eleven . . . He claims to have spent the whole evening at the Station Arms . . . In answer to the routine questions he stated that he remembered passing the walls of a "big house" but that he had noticed nothing. He had not, to the best of his recollection, seen a red Mini saloon . . . The witness was nervous and gave the impression that he was not being entirely truthful . . . Blah, Blah, Blah, W. H. Pasco, Detective Sergeant.'

W. H. Pascoe, Detective Sergeant, had more to say on another sheet: 'John Trew, landlord of the Station Arms, confirmed that Brandt had been in his bar on Thursday evening but said that he had not stayed the whole evening. At about nine forty-five he had left in company with Lena Rowe, a known prostitute.'

Wycliffe decided to talk to Brandt himself; he would call in at the fairground on his way to see Sidney Bryce. As he was leaving he asked the duty constable, 'Any news of Mr Gill?'

'Not yet, sir.'

Wycliffe grumbled to himself. 'Why the hell can't he report in like anybody else?' In fact, Jimmy Gill suffered from the same complaint as his chief, a tendency to play a lone hand.

It was Wednesday, half-day closing for the shops,

and, presumably for that reason, the fair had started early. Instead of skirting the ground, Wycliffe walked through it in search of Frederick Brandt. A fair in daylight is like a woman in curlers, but a few youths and girls were conscientiously trying to whoop it up without much success. The dodgems were doing business and so was a contrivance, new since Wycliffe's day, which swept rotating carloads of its victims at the ends of long poles through a seemingly unpredictable and hazardous trajectory. To judge from the screams it was money well spent.

But for Wycliffe the heart and the lungs of the fair were missing, the giant steam traction-engines and the steam organ. As a child it had been enough for him to stand looking up at the spinning fly-wheel of Lord Nelson or The Gladiator. He remembered the twisted brass supports for the canopy, like sticks of barley sugar; the gleaming cross-head darting to and fro; the oily, steamy, wash-day smell, and the ground under foot trembling to the rhythm of the monster. 'You see that round thing in front, driven by the belt; that's the dynamo – it supplies electricity to the whole fair.' His father was as captivated as he was, and they would stand together, spellbound. If they tired, there was always the steam organ with its posturing cavaliers and pirouetting ladies, banks of brass trumpets and, above all, its drenching cascade of sound. All gone.

He made his way to the caravans which bordered the ground on two sides. Most of them seemed to be deserted, but a woman, sitting on the steps of one of them peeling potatoes, directed him. 'Brandt? The little white van. What's he done? The bogeys was in there this morning nearly an hour.'

Brandt's IQ must have been well down in the double figures; he had the build of a young gorilla and nothing to keep his hair from his eyebrows. The door of the caravan was open and Wycliffe found him lying on one of the bunks, turning the pages of an American comic. The caravan was filthy. He looked at Wycliffe, vaguely at first, then with dawning intelligence. 'Are you a scuffer?' He dropped the paper on the floor and sat up.

'Where is your girl-friend?'

'Marge? She's working – on the darts.'

'And you?'

'You what?' He looked uncomprehending.

Wycliffe sat himself on the opposite bunk. 'Why aren't you working?'

'Oh, I work when they shut down: cleaning up, that's my job – and helping Mr Oates with the maintenance.'

'So you go to the pub in the evenings on your own.'

He looked sheepish. 'You got to do something, and Marge don't mind, not if I . . .'

'But she would mind if she knew you'd picked up a trollop like Lena Rowe?'

He nodded. 'That's why I never said anything to your . . .' He broke off, confused. 'She was here.'

It was like taking money from a blind man, but this near-idiot had already put two people in hospital and himself in gaol, so what price freedom?

'Where did you take her? – Lena, I mean.'

It was rather a question of where she had taken him, but it amounted to the same thing.

'Not far from the boozer there's a big house with a wall and in the wall there's doors for garages . . .'

'Well?'

'There's a bus shelter; we went in there.'

'What time was this?'

He thought for a moment. 'I don't rightly know; it were after I left the boozer. She wanted me to be quick because she had another fella lined up she said.' He grinned. 'God! She was a scrubber! She wanted three quid – three bloody quid for . . .'

'When did you see the car?'

'The car?'

'The red Mini.'

'Oh, that. It come out of one of the garages an' drove off at a lick down the road.'

'Towards the town or away from it?'

'What?'

'Towards the pub or the other way?'

'Oh, the other way, away from the boozer. I said to the bird, "He's in more of a bleeding hurry than you are!" I said that to her.'

'He?'

'The driver.'

'There was a man driving the car?'

'Well, there would be, wouldn't there?'

'Not a woman?'

'Oh, I don't know about that; I couldn't see.'

'But you saw the red car.'

'Oh yes, I saw it pass under the light. It was a red Mini.'

'And that was all you saw?'

'I was busy.' He paused then added with concern, 'You won't tell Marge? She'd kill me.'

More likely that he would end up by killing her without meaning to. 'I won't tell her unless I have to; but you behave yourself.'

He was glad to escape into the air, to get away from the odour of stale sweat and burnt fat. At times like this he thanked God that he was not a parson, nor any of the species of social workers spawned in town halls. He had only to catch crooks, not to try to patch up lives.

So it looked as though Zel had told, at least, part of the truth. The red Mini had been driven from Boslow at about the time she said; but the question remained – by whom? If, as Zel said, her mother had driven the car away, why had she not gone to the station to catch her train? If Caroline really had left Boslow alive then this told strongly in favour of Matthew Bryce. Had she been stopped by someone on her way to the station? By her murderer? So far it seemed that only George Bryce knew of her true destination that night; he had made the appointment.

Wycliffe was tempted to go back to his headquarters for news of Jimmy Gill, for it seemed that the cards were stacking against George; but he decided to see Sidney Bryce first.

Bryce Brothers' head office was in the square, above a large hardware shop which belonged to the firm. Sidney's office overlooked the square. It was a modern office, functional to the point of being spartan. No sign of the Edwardian banker here. He received Wycliffe with cordiality but without effusion and got right down to business. Against his will, Wycliffe was favourably impressed.

'I expect that you would prefer to ask me questions.'

Wycliffe found himself becoming genial. 'The obvious one, I'm afraid: have you any idea who killed your sister-in-law?'

'None.'

Wycliffe nodded. 'Do you think it possible that she was killed to prevent the sale of your firm to BTC?'

Sidney opened a cigar box and offered it across to the chief superintendent.

'No thanks; I prefer a pipe.'

Bryce nipped off the end of his cigar and lit it. 'The answer to your question is, "Definitely not". It is quite true that now Caroline is dead the deal will not go through; it is also true that my brother Matt was bitterly opposed to the sale. But Matt would never . . .' He broke off with an expressive gesture. 'Matt is totally incapable of violence.'

A soft buzzing came from the intercom on his desk and he flicked a button. 'No calls please, Mrs Grose.'

Wycliffe was filling his pipe. 'In my experience, even the most gentle of men may be goaded into violence; it is often a question of touching the tender spot. We all seem to have one.'

Sidney was thoughtful. 'The tender spot – yes, you may be right. But for Matt, despite all his concern for the business, that would not be it.'

'His wife's infidelity?'

Bryce shook his head vigorously. 'He was almost indifferent; he accepted the situation, which had been going on for years.'

It was refreshing not to have to spell everything out. Bryce assumed that he had done his homework, that he was acquainted with the family skeletons.

'If Matt has a tender spot, as you call it, it is Zel. If someone harmed or threatened Zel . . .'

'But Zel's mother could hardly be in that category.' Wycliffe was bland.

'No-one would think so, certainly.' Sidney Bryce was toying with his cigar which had gone out. Wycliffe was sure that he wished to convey something without putting it into words. 'All the same . . .'

'Perhaps there was too little difference in their ages. A girl of sixteen or seventeen can be competition for a mother of thirty-four.'

Bryce made a curious gesture of distaste. 'A woman jealous of her own daughter! It seems incredible. But you are right: Caroline was jealous of Zel.' He looked at his dead cigar and dropped it into the ashtray. 'I am a bachelor and I know very little of these things; but I would have thought that any normal woman . . .'

Wycliffe wanted to say no more than would keep him talking.

'How did this . . . this jealousy show itself?'

'In a hundred ways. Of course, she was too clever to let Matt see. In any case, Matt is not very observant; sometimes he hardly sees what is going on under his very nose. I had never realized that a woman could be so unfeeling.' He held up his hands in a helpless gesture as though words failed him. 'She would allow Zel to plan something for days or even weeks – some trivial thing which would give the child pleasure, an outing, a school trip, a picnic – then the day before or even on the day she would pretend to know nothing about it. She would laugh and say, "But my dear girl, whatever gave you the idea that I would allow such a thing? Really! You are too absurd!" ' He broke off, realizing that he was betraying himself. 'I'm sorry. You can see that I feel strongly on the subject.'

'That is quite natural,' Wycliffe said; but he wondered if it was. In the few minutes he had been in the room he seemed to have found Sidney's tender spot. Obviously he lived vicariously through the lives of his brother's family. A common enough phenomenon with maiden aunts – but bachelor uncles? Was it a more sinister situation?

'I can see that you disliked your sister-in-law.'

'That is an understatement.'

'Which makes it all the more strange that you entered into a business arrangement with her to frustrate your brother's wishes.'

'You mean, over the deal with BTC?' Bryce seemed surprised. 'That was quite a different matter. In any case there was no arrangement as you call it. I did not conspire with Matt's wife behind his back; it happened, for once, that we were in agreement.' He sat back in his chair and recovered his self-possession as his thoughts turned back to business. 'The point is that Matt's ideas are fifty years out of date. Our firm was built on two principles, diversification of investment and paternalism toward our employees – both perfectly valid in their time but now, dead as the dodo. Nowadays one has to specialize – to narrow the scope of one's business and concentrate on being more efficient than one's competitors; and in labour relations one has to recognize that there is no obvious identity of interest and use the machinery of collective bargaining. BTC would have done these things and the result would have been not only continued prosperity now, but an assurance for the future.' He stopped speaking, gazing at the blotter in front of him. 'One has a conscience in these matters.'

It was a new thought for Wycliffe.

'Your sister-in-law had no doubts about selling?'

'Doubts? On the contrary, she was delighted to be rid of her investment in the firm, particularly on such favourable terms.'

Wycliffe thought it was time for a lull. If you are fishing it is a mistake to be too eager. He smoked his pipe and looked out of the window. He could see over the grey slate roofs of the houses on the lower side of the square to the high ground above East Treen; a field of yellow stubble, where the corn had been harvested, caught the sun and glowed like Van Gogh sunflowers. Few people can sustain silence for long and Bryce was no exception.

'Perhaps I should tell you that if the deal had gone

through, Caroline would have taken cash for her holding and left Boslow.'

'She told you?'

'Yes.'

A tap at the door and a grey-haired, motherly soul put her head round it. 'What is it, Mrs Grose?' Bryce was irritable.

'I know you don't want to be disturbed, Mr Sidney, but there's a call for the chief superintendent.'

It was Jimmy Gill. 'They told me you'd gone to see brother Sid. It's probably not wise to say much over the phone but I thought you ought to know. It looks as though the car spent Thursday night there.'

'Is that all?'

'It's possible that we've got the weapon.'

'You want me to make a decision?'

'Among other things – yes.'

'I'll be right back.'

Wycliffe dropped the receiver. Bryce was studying some papers on his desk. 'A development?'

'Of a sort. I'm afraid that we shall have to postpone our conversation; but you have been most helpful.'

Mutual assurances of goodwill before parting. Bryce came downstairs to see him off. Lovely flannel to delight the heart of Mr Bellings.

'I'd better start with the cleaning woman, Gerty Pearce. According to Birkett, she's a regular Mrs Mop: on the right side of fifty, talkative but not malicious.' Jimmy Gill sat in Wycliffe's office, smoking one of his cheroots. Wycliffe had considered lighting a pipe but the air was thick already.

'She was there when Caroline Bryce came on Tuesday afternoon – early afternoon, she says it was. George took Caroline into the sitting-room and they talked for half-an-hour. The old girl heard nothing that was said but she doesn't think they could have been quarrelling.'

'Where did Caroline leave the car?'

'According to Gerty she always left it outside the boathouse, even when, as she put it, "they was going steady like". Before Caroline's visit on the Tuesday Gerty hadn't seen her for several weeks, though up till then "she'd been in and out like she lived here".'

'Has she any suggestion as to why that changed?'

'She thinks George got tired of her when he found the other. "Most men prefer lamb to mutton if they can get it" was Gerty's way of putting it.'

It was refreshing not to have to spell everything out.

'Anything else from Gerty?'

'Only that the girl, Zel, was always hanging about the place.'

'Doing what?'

'Gerty says she was spying on her mother.'

'What about the boathouse?'

Gill rubbed the bristles on his five-o'clock shadow with the flat of his hand. 'With one exception the tyre tracks are from one car, presumably George's MG.'

'And the exception?'

'The red Mini.'

'You seem sure of yourself.'

'Not me. Dr Bell of Forensic was at Divisional HQ so I asked him to come over. He had been working on the Mini and he is in no doubt that the track belongs to the off-side front wheel. He thinks somebody had tried to obliterate the marks but missed one. It's recent, and he says it could have been made on Thursday night.'

'So we conclude that the Mini spent Thursday night in George's boathouse, is that it?'

'It looks like it, but I suppose the question is where Caroline spent that night.'

'And whether she was dead or alive.'

'Franks thinks she was dead.'

'But Franks would be the first to admit that he couldn't sustain that in court; it's no more than an informed guess.' Wycliffe pushed the window wider to get rid of the smoke. 'I don't know what gives you the idea that those damn things are less dangerous than cigarettes; they nearly kill me.'

Chief Inspector Gill looked at his half-smoked cheroot in surprise. 'These? They're mild as mother's milk – they tell you that on the telly. But if they offend . . .' With a dramatic gesture he pitched the butt out of the window. 'Now, where were we?'

'I was on the point of asking you what George Bryce had to say about all this?'

'He couldn't say anything; he wasn't there. Apparently he hasn't been back since you saw him leave this morning.'

Wycliffe shrugged. 'I suppose he could have taken fright. Anyway, what was that you said about a weapon?'

'It's not certain; but lying in a corner of the boathouse there's a pile of scrap including some lengths of lead piping. One of the pieces, about eighteen inches long, has a ragged end and there were one or two hairs adhering to it. Forensic are going to let you have a report.'

Wycliffe nodded. 'Did you check on George's story – what he was supposed to have been doing on Thursday night?'

'Birkett saw the two chaps, Scoble and Miller. Both of them say he was with them until one in the morning on some sort of jag. They left him at Whitecross, about seven miles from Treen, and they were a bit worried about him driving home because he was high. Of course, they may be lying; Birkett is checking it out.'

'Anything else?'

'Nothing.' Gill looked at his chief with a sardonic grin. 'How long does Georgie have to absent himself before you put out a call?'

Wycliffe glowered. 'All right! I'm no more anxious than the next one to make a fool of myself.'

'What about a quick one before dinner?'

It was a quarter past six. Through the rear window of the van Wycliffe could see the estuary fringed with broad stretches of black mud. Low tide. Two concrete slipways reached out from opposite banks like fingers, making it possible for the ferry to continue running. He picked up a bundle of reports. 'Give me ten minutes with these and I'll join you.'

The reports summarized the results of house to house inquiries, but only one item interested Wycliffe.

A motor bike had been parked at the end of Station Road, a few yards from the back entrance to Boslow, between eleven and one on the night of the murder. The householder, a widow living alone, had noticed it when she put the cat out before going to bed and she had been awakened by someone trying to start it just after one o'clock. She remembered that the machine had a bright red petrol tank and this fact had enabled the owner to be traced; he was John Evans, an apprentice at the boatyard. He said that he had parked his bike there while he walked with his girl-friend on the river bank. Between eleven and one? It sounded thin.

He walked over to the hotel and joined Gill in the lounge bar of the hotel. A red-head in a white sweater with plenty of uplift and slim-fit black pants was perched on a bar stood sipping gin. Wycliffe did not recognize her until she spoke – Margaret Haynes. 'I thought I might see you here.'

She was chummy, Wycliffe was distant. 'You wanted to see me?'

She slid off the stool, her eyes on Jimmy Gill. 'It seemed like a good idea.'

Wycliffe bought drinks and they took them to a window seat away from the bar. Apart from the barman they had the place to themselves.

'I've been talking to Gerty Pearce, she's been telling me . . .' She was staring at her glass, running her index finger round the rim, determined to be interesting. 'Before you get any ideas about George you ought to know that I spent Thursday night with him.'

'At his place?'

'Of course.'

'You didn't think to tell me that this morning.'

'You didn't ask me.'

'Mr Bryce told me that he spent the night alone.'

She shrugged.

'Where is he now?' Gill put the question.

She gave him her full attention before answering. 'Isn't he back yet?'

'Back from where?'

'I've no idea. I know he was off somewhere. I expect it was about money; it usually is.'

'What time did you meet him on Thursday?'

'I went to his place in the evening, but he wasn't there so I decided to wait. I must have fallen asleep . . .'

'You have a key?'

'No need; it's never locked.'

'So you were there when Bryce came back?'

'Yes.'

'What time?'

'Midnight, one o'clock, I haven't a clue really.'

'So you must have seen Caroline Bryce?'

She looked suspicious. 'I don't get you.'

'You didn't see her?'

'No, of course I didn't!'

Wycliffe was unimpressed by the story. 'You will be required to make a statement.'

The blue eyes regarded him with practised candour. 'Why not?'

'What time did you leave Foundry House on Friday morning?'

She drained her glass and put it down with an expectant glance at Jimmy Gill. He got up. 'Same again?' She followed him with her eyes as he went to the bar but she answered Wycliffe's question.

'It must have been about six; there are no clocks that work there but I got home before Mum and Dad were about.'

Wycliffe wondered what Mum and Dad thought about their daughter and what they said. Probably it was too late to say anything. 'If you come to my HQ caravan first thing tomorrow morning one of my officers will take your statement.'

Gill came back with the drinks. 'I gather you work for Morley?'

'I type his letters for him when he's down here.'

Gill grimaced. 'Funny job for a sex-kitten like you. I thought the Right Hon was all against what comes naturally.'

She grinned; this was the kind of talk she understood. 'He doesn't come naturally or otherwise when I'm about; I just type his letters and mind my own business.' She laughed across at Wycliffe. 'Are all your policemen like him?'

Gill looked like a lecherous toad. 'He's not married, is he?'

'Not as far as I know.'

'And not interested?'

'If you're trying to say he's a queer, you may be right; but it's no good asking me.' She sipped her drink. 'Satisfied?'

'Perhaps. What does he think about your goings on with George Bryce?'

'I've never asked him; it's none of his business, is it?'

When she had finished her drink she got up. 'See you around!' She walked away from them, wiggling her bottom as she went.

Gill sighed. 'Like a victory roll! What a dolly!'

It was one of the chief inspector's assets that he could get answers to questions which few policemen would dare ask. He emptied his glass. 'Do you think she was telling the truth?'

'I doubt if she'd recognize truth if she saw it,' Wycliffe growled.

The gong sounded and they went in to dinner.

6

Thursday morning; forty-eight hours after the ferry-men had fished Caroline Bryce's body out of the water. It seemed to Wycliffe that he had been talking to and thinking about Bryces for much longer.

On his desk were two reports, one from Dr Bell, head of Forensic and the other from the pathologist, Dr Franks. Dr Bell confirmed that a few hairs taken from the lead piping found in the boathouse were human and that they matched the hair of the dead woman. Dried mud removed from the treads of the wrecked Mini had come from the floor of the boat-house. An examination of the clothing, especially of the shoes, taken from the body, suggested that immersion had lasted less than four days rather than more. In other words, Bell was of the opinion that the body had been placed in the water on Friday night and not Thursday, welcome confirmation of Franks' con-clusion based on his study of the body itself. A longish section of the report dealt with finger-prints, but only one reference interested Wycliffe: an unidentified set of prints found on the underside of the steering wheel of the Mini. These prints were unknown to Criminal Records and they did not match those of anyone involved in the case so far. Dr Bell was prepared to say that the prints were 'quite recent'.

Wycliffe was growing concerned. There was still no news of George Bryce and almost hourly the case against him was being strengthened. The previous evening, reluctantly, he had circulated Bryce's description: 'Wanted for questioning . . .' Now it certainly looked as though he had done a bunk. Margaret Haynes' testimony was in his favour but, unsupported, it was not worth much. Her statement would be checked with great care but it might be impossible to confirm two vital points, the time he had returned to Foundry House and whether she had spent the night with him as she said. Which reminded Wycliffe that she had not arrived to make her statement. Probably she was still in bed. He reached for the telephone. 'Send a car to pick up Margaret Haynes; she's the daughter of the golf "pro" and lives at the Club. She has volunteered to make a statement and she may be on her way here; tell the driver to look out for a red-head, nineteen or twenty years old . . .'

He dropped the telephone. Through the window he saw a uniformed policeman go to one of the parked cars and drive off. His headquarters had grown: there were two caravans now and a temporary fence round them enclosing enough ground to park four or five vehicles. The fence was Jimmy Gill's answer to the over-inquisitiveness of the press. It was raining and the ground was becoming soggy with a chain of puddles spreading across it. He could sit and stare out of the window with an almost blank mind indefinitely. He forced his thoughts back to the case. It seemed that Caroline's Mini had spent Thursday night in George's boathouse. With or without his knowledge? And where was Caroline? Had she got cold feet about her London trip and driven to Foundry House instead of to the station? She would have found the house empty; perhaps she had decided to wait. It was just possible that she had met the Haynes girl there. Then

George had returned, making a very incongruous threesome. Wycliffe sighed; it was not impossible. He would have to get the truth out of the Haynes girl.

Assume for the moment there had been a row and George had killed her. He had to dispose of the body but the tide was already well into the ebb and the river was the obvious place. He might reasonably have decided to wait until the next night . . .

He was not enthusiastic about the theory and more interesting thoughts jostled each other on the fringes of his mind: words, names, brief but vividly re-collected incidents, odd disjointed phrases – scarcely thoughts at all. He found himself saying: 'It all started a long time ago; it is not a bit of use considering the events of a day or of a week and expecting to under-stand them. These people had been in Treen for a long time, they had grown up there, and their jealousies, their spites, their loves and their hates had grown with them.'

'So what?'

His telephone rang.

'There's a man on the line, sir; a Mr Eva, a grocer with a little shop on the outskirts of St Austell. He thinks he had George Bryce in his shop yesterday evening.'

'Put him through and listen in.'

Fortunately Mr Eva was lucid and sure of his ground. 'This man certainly answered the description in the paper . . . No, we didn't watch TV last night . . . No, I don't know Mr Bryce by sight. I know his brother, Mr Sidney, through Rotary . . .' He must have been speaking from the shop: Wycliffe could hear the noise of a cash register from time to time. 'Yes, he came into the shop just before closing time – about ten minutes to six . . . Quite a lot of stuff – about five pounds' worth, mostly canned goods and cigarettes . . . Yes, he was alone; of course there could have been somebody waiting for him in the car outside.' Mr Eva interrupted himself to tell someone that the large packet had gone up to four shillings. 'No, I didn't notice what sort of car it was . . . I don't know about nervous, but he seemed to be in a hurry . . . My place is on the A390 about a mile on the Treen side of the town . . . Yes, I'm pretty sure he was going towards the town.'

Wycliffe thanked him and said that he would send someone to take his statement. 'Looks as though he's holed up somewhere not too far away.' This to the duty constable who had listened in. 'Get on to Information Room and ask them to raise Chief Inspector Gill on his car radio. Pass on the message; he'll know what to do – and ask him to meet me here sometime before lunch. Got that?'

At this time of year there must be hundreds of untenanted furnished cottages and caravans within a radius of ten miles where a man could live comfortably if he had food. And at six o'clock the previous evening Bryce had been buying stocks of food a few miles away. The chances were that he had come back to Foundry House and spotted the police before they spotted him. Then he doubled back, bought provisions, and now would be sitting pretty until his supplies ran out. The only thing was a search of likely premises.

The constable who had been sent to bring in Margaret Haynes returned. 'Miss Haynes left home early this morning and her mother has no idea where she has gone.'

'What does she call early?'

'Before nine, sir. Mrs Haynes took her daughter a

cup of tea at eight o'clock but when she went to her bedroom just before nine the girl was gone.'

'Gone? Had she taken anything with her?'

'Only the clothes she was wearing.'

'So it looks as though she intends to come back. If she was going to join Bryce she would have taken a change of clothes at least.'

Wycliffe was depressed; he felt that he was losing his grip on the case. The weather hardly helped; rain was sweeping up the estuary driven before a rising wind which buffeted the caravan so that it shuddered on its supports. He stared out at the dissolving landscape in a mood of gloomy petulance, feeling that he was overdue for a stroke of luck.

And luck of a sort came his way. A woman, a permanent resident on a caravan site a few miles down the coast, reported to the police a 'suspicious character' who had moved into one of the many unoccupied vans on the site.

The same rainstorm which helped to depress Wycliffe drove over the desolate caravan site, its teeth sharpened by sand blown from the beach. Two policemen in heavy blue raincoats, their collars turned up, stood by one of the vans; one knocked with his knuckles on the door. The curtains were drawn and the van seemed to be deserted. After an interval the policeman knocked again and this time there was a movement inside and a voice said, 'Who is it?'

'Police! Open up!'

And in due course the door was opened and George Bryce stood there gazing at them rather stupidly. He was bleary-eyed and unshaven, in shirt sleeves and slippers; a very different figure from the dandified man-about-town Wycliffe had met at Foundry House.

'Is this your caravan, sir?'

'It's not actually mine, no.' He seemed to collect his wits. 'But the owner is a friend of mine.'

'And you have his permission to use it?'

The second policeman cut in. 'You're George Bryce!'

He made no attempt to deny it.

'We must ask you to accompany us to the nearest police station, sir.'

Bryce gazed at them with a puzzled frown as though he could not be sure they were real. 'Why?'

'To answer some questions.'

Wycliffe heard the news by telephone. 'He's at Division now, sir. Shall we send him along to you?'

Looking out of the window at the rain-soaked world he was on the point of saying 'Yes' when it occurred to him that there is always a risk of treating human beings like commodities once you have a little power over them. 'I'll come to Division.'

He was driven over and at Divisional Headquarters they found him a room and a stenographer. Bryce was brought in. He had shaved and smartened himself up but he looked older, less sleek, than when Wycliffe had seen him the previous day.

'Smoke if you want to.'

Bryce got out his cigarettes and lit one; but all the time his eyes were fixed, not on Wycliffe, but on the stenographer who happened to be a seventeen-stone constable. Perhaps he was afraid of physical violence.

'Would you like to get in touch with your lawyer?'

'I haven't got one.'

'You could get one.'

'No.'

Wycliffe cautioned him. The room was lit by a glaring fluorescent tube in the ceiling and the only window looked out on a blank wall across a narrow alley; the kind of room which would have driven Wycliffe mad had he been forced to work or live in it.

'Yesterday evening you visited a grocer's shop near St Austell where you bought a lot of tinned food?'

Bryce nodded.

'Earlier you had gone to your house, found the police there and cleared out – Why?'

Bryce shifted uncomfortably in his chair. 'I was afraid that I might be arrested.'

'Why should you be arrested?'

'I don't suppose you sent your men there for fun; you must have thought you had something against me.' His eyes were still on the constable who was writing everything down.

'But what was the point of running away? You must have realized that you would have been picked up sooner or later.'

'I thought you might find out you were wrong.'

'You thought that we might decide that someone else had killed your sister-in-law?'

'I suppose so – yes.'

'What about Margaret Haynes?'

Bryce stopped with a cigarette halfway to his lips. 'What about her?'

'When did you last see her?'

'Yesterday morning. You were there.'

'And when did you last speak to her – on the telephone perhaps?'

'I don't understand.'

'I think you do. When did you tell her to come to me with the tale that she spent Thursday night at Foundry House?'

Little drops of perspiration were running down Bryce's nose. 'I didn't tell her to do that; but it's the truth.'

'It's a lie, of course. If she was there she would have seen Caroline Bryce.'

George Bryce was badly scared and his eyes went from the constable to Wycliffe and back again, never still. 'I don't understand what you are getting at.'

'All right, I'll be more explicit. Caroline Bryce spent Thursday night and all day Friday in your boathouse, in her Mini; she was dead.'

Bryce would have interrupted but Wycliffe went on. 'On Friday night at high tide you put her dead body in the water having weighted it with something which you wired to her ankle; then you drove her car to the quarry above the town and pushed it over the edge of the scrap heap.' He paused and regarded Bryce with mild curiosity. 'If you didn't kill her, why did you go to all this trouble?'

Bryce's face was white and his voice was scarcely audible. 'You see how it is; I don't stand a chance.' He was silent for a moment then he added, 'I didn't kill her.'

'The weapon with which she was killed was found in your boathouse – one of the pieces of scrap lead piping which lie there. I am going to charge you, Mr Bryce. It is up to you whether the charge is murder or being an accessory . . .'

'I didn't kill her. I'll tell you what happened.'

'Very well; but I'll repeat the caution.'

Bryce took a grubby handkerchief from his pocket and wiped the sweat from his face. 'Christ! It's hot in here.'

'Take your time.'

'I came back on Thursday night – Friday morning, as I told you; I'd had a few drinks so I left the old bus outside the shed and padded off to bed. Next morning I got up when Gerty arrived, about eleven, with the father and mother of a hangover. I pottered about the house a bit. It was pouring with rain so I thought I might as well put the car under cover.' He stopped speaking and took a deep breath. 'When I opened the shed I saw her car. I thought it was bloody queer but it didn't bother me too much till I saw she was in it . . .'

'Was she in the passenger seat or the driver's?'

'The driver's. She was wearing the safety harness, all strapped in, and her head was bent forward on her chest.'

'What did you do?'

'Do? I got out, shut the doors and hared back to the house. I wanted to think.'

'Without finding out whether she was dead or not?'

He was silent for a moment, fiddling with his sideboards. 'She was dead all right; I made sure of that . . .'

'How long? You're a doctor; how long had she been dead?'

Bryce was obviously afraid of a trap: his eyes never left Wycliffe's face. 'I didn't examine her thoroughly; she was all slumped up. In any case the circumstances . . .'

'How long?'

'In my opinion – for what it is worth – about twelve to fifteen hours.'

'Say between nine and midnight the previous night?'

He nodded. 'About that.'

'Which lets you out.'

Bryce said nothing.

'Did you come to any conclusions as to the cause of death?'

'It seemed obvious: her head was bent forward and

the hair had been parted at the base of the skull as though to display the injury.'

'Which was?'

'A depressed fracture of the occipital region of the skull.'

'Any blood?'

'No.'

'So you went back to the house. What did you do then?'

He dabbed his upper lip with his handkerchief. 'I had to think.'

'It didn't occur to you to inform the police?'

'Of course it did; but with my reputation in this place I'm a sitting duck for anybody who wants to set me up.'

'Who would want to do that?'

'I've no idea but, evidently, somebody did.'

'Your brother Matt?'

A quick look. 'Not a chance! Matt will open the window to let out a bloody wasp which has just stung him.'

'Why did you have to leave Boslow?'

Bryce shrugged.

'Was it because you were sleeping with Caroline.'

'That's what they say, isn't it?'

'But what do you say?'

Bryce was silent for a while. The muffled sound of traffic reached them in the claustrophobic little room like sounds from another world. 'I'm going to tell you the truth even though it could be twisted against me.'

'I'm not going to twist anything and you would certainly be wise to tell the truth.'

Bryce played with his sideboards, pulling at the soft hairs. 'Matt wasn't unduly bothered about Caroline and me. I'm not saying that it didn't go against the grain at first, but he got used to it. He knew he couldn't give her what she wanted – what she needed, and I'm not only talking about sex. Caroline needed affection, she needed people to like her and to show that they liked her; but Matt is incapable of any show of emotion even to people he really loves. You may not believe it but in the end it suited Matt to have me round – keep it in the family, so to speak.'

'Then why did he kick you out?'

'It was over Zel.'

'Zel?'

'He thought that I had seduced her.'

'And had you?'

'No, I bloody well hadn't! Barely nubile girls are not my line.'

'All right, go on.'

'The poor kid fell for me. You know how adolescent girls can get a thing about an older man without any encouragement. And Zel got no encouragement from me. Perhaps she was jealous of her mother and wanted to take her place. Psychology was never my strong suit, but whatever it was it was bloody embarrassing . . .'

'Well?'

Bryce made an irritable movement. 'Do I have to draw a bloody picture? She made life complicated, always coming into my room in her little nylon nightie. Poor little bastard, it was pathetic. I tried to make her see sense, I reasoned with her; but it didn't work.'

'Did you try telling her mother?'

'Like hell. Caroline could be sadistic with the kid. I dared not risk it.'

'So what happened?'

'Matt got wind of it.'

'You explained?'

'I didn't get a lot of chance.'

'What about Zel?'

He hesitated. 'I'm not sure, but I think Zel told her father in the first place.'

'That you had made advances to her?'

He nodded. 'I suppose it was her way of getting her own back.' He lit another cigarette.

In the last half-hour he had succeeded in making Wycliffe more kindly disposed towards him.

'After you came to Foundry House she continued to visit you. Did she still try to get you to make love to her?'

'It wasn't the same.' He seemed to have difficulty in choosing his words. 'Her attitude to me was almost patronizing. I don't know how else to describe it. And she spied on me and on her mother. She still comes and goes as the whim takes her and one hardly knows when she's there and when she isn't; but one way and another there isn't much she doesn't know about what's gone on in my house over the past two years.'

'You don't discourage her visits?'

Bryce raised his hands in a gesture of helplessness. 'What good would it do?'

Wycliffe stood up and walked over to the window; by putting his face close to the pane of glass he could peer up at a narrow band of dun-coloured sky with clouds like smoke chasing each other across it. He filled his pipe and lit it, taking time over the ritual. Bryce sat in silence, his hands clasped round one knee.

'What about Clement Morley?'

'What about him?'

'See much of him?'

'Not more than I can help. I've no room for his sort and he hates my guts.'

'Why?'

'For one thing, I suppose, my affair with his half-sister would hardly do his Sunday school campaign any good.'

'But he would hardly have murdered Caroline to spite you.'

Bryce grimaced with distaste. 'I suppose not; but I could believe almost anything of that greasy bastard. Caroline had something on him.'

'On Morley?'

He nodded. 'She knew something.'

'You've no idea what?'

'Not a clue; she could be close when she wanted to be.'

'Do you think she was blackmailing him?'

Bryce hesitated. 'I think she probably threatened him from time to time. She loved to have something she could hold over you, and when she had she didn't let you forget it.'

'And what did she hold over you? Was it the fact that you owed her money?'

He did not argue. 'All right, I admit it. You can't say I'm not being straight with you.'

Wycliffe lit his pipe and waited until it was drawing nicely. 'Let's get back to Friday night, when you put her body in the river.'

'It was as you said: I had to wait for the top of the tide because of the mud . . .'

'And the car?'

'After I'd dealt with the body I drove the car up to the edge of the quarry and pushed it over.'

'There's a track in on the level of the quarry floor – why didn't you simply drive in?'

He fiddled with his sideboards. 'There's a cottage too near for comfort. In any case I had some idea of making the car less noticeable by smashing it on a pile of scrap.'

'And then you walked back?'

'Yes.'

'Meet anybody?'

'No.'

There was little more to be got out of Bryce. He repeated that it had been he who broke off the affair with Caroline; which was probably true, though a man like George Bryce would never admit to having received marching orders from a woman.

After he had signed his statement, Wycliffe had him charged and taken into custody.

It was after three when Wycliffe arrived back at his Treen headquarters, and it was still raining. Jimmy Gill was sitting in the gloomy little office going through reports.

'Any news of the girl?'

'Her mother rang up; she's getting worried.'

Wycliffe stood by the window, staring out over the grey waste of the estuary. 'She didn't go to join Bryce, that's certain.'

Gill tilted his chair at a dangerous angle. 'I wish she had.'

Wycliffe got out his pipe. 'There's no reason to think . . .'

And Gill interrupted, 'None at all; all the same I shall feel happier when we hear that she's back with Mum.'

'So shall I,' Wycliffe agreed.

'If she told somebody she was coming here to make a statement . . .' Gill broke off and allowed his chair to come back to a safer angle. 'Anyway, what did George have to say for himself?'

Wycliffe told him.

'You sound as though you believed him.'

Wycliffe nodded. 'I think I do.'

'Which leaves us with the other two brothers and with Morley. What about Matt?'

Wycliffe studied the bowl of his pipe. 'Everybody I've spoken to so far except Joyce Boon has been only too anxious to convince me that Matt wouldn't kill a cockroach. In any case, what motive did he have last week which he hasn't had for years?'

'It would have to be something to do with Zel.'

'But what? What has changed? The girl is growing up, legally she's an adult, certainly she's more capable of standing up for herself now than she has ever been.'

Gill nodded. 'I see that: all the same, Matt is a credible suspect – murderers are rarely logical. Matt had the opportunity. He could have killed his wife before she left Boslow, driven the car to Foundry House and left it in the boathouse with the body in it . . .'

Wycliffe sighed. 'Save it, Jimmy! You may be right but it doesn't get us anywhere. We need to know more about these people. They've got a long history here in Treen, they're well dug in.' He came to a sudden decision. 'I'm going to see Margaret Haynes' parents.'

The girl's continued absence was troubling him. She had seemed ready enough to make a statement but she had not come.

7

Wycliffe drove to the Haynes' bungalow, a pleasant place on rising ground behind the club-house, backed by trees. From the terrace in front of the house it would have been possible to see the sea but for the steady rain like a grey curtain over the estuary. Mrs Haynes took him into the sitting-room, its once gay chintzes faded by the sun. She was a red-head like her daughter and still not much over forty. She wore a tight black skirt and a frilly white blouse with a plunging 'V'. She was at once concerned and petulant.

'I really can't understand her, Mr Wycliffe! She takes no notice of me; and if her father says a word she flares up. We sent her to a good school and when she said she wanted to do secretarial training we paid for her to go to a special college . . .

'Of course, she never kept a job for more than a month. It isn't that we mind about the money, but a girl should do something, don't you think? Then when Ricky – that's my husband – when Ricky put in a word for her with Mr Clement Morley and she got the job, things seemed to be better for a time. Of course, it's only when he's down here, but it's better than nothing.

'I mean, she's never home! I used to lie awake at nights listening for her to come in, but I had to stop it . . . Ricky said . . .'

'How old is your daughter, Mrs Haynes?'

'She was nineteen last month.'

'Does she ever stay out all night?'

'Sometimes she spends the night with friends but she always tells me if she is going to do that.'

'You have no idea where she might have gone?'

The rather stupid face wrinkled into lines of worry. 'Why, no! Apparently she was due to go to Mr Morley's at two o'clock. He telephoned at about half-past to ask where she was. That made it worse because she's never let him down before. I suppose I wouldn't have been bothered then if it hadn't been for your policeman coming here this morning. What do you want her for? I mean, she hasn't done anything . . . ?' Her manner was blended of fear and aggression.

Wycliffe tried to be reassuring. 'Nothing! She was going to help us with our inquiries into Mrs Bryce's death . . .'

'But how could she? She only went near the place once in a while.'

'She was a friend of George Bryce.'

'Not a friend; she just knew him.'

'Try to think back to last Thursday, Mrs Haynes. Did Margaret come home that night?'

'Come home? Of course she came home! What are you suggesting?'

'You said that she sometimes stayed with friends.'

She was mollified. 'Yes, but not Thursday . . .'

'You are quite sure?'

She pulled her skirt over her knees. 'I'm quite sure as it happens; that was the night Ricky was so ill. I had to get up to look after him and I happened to look into Margaret's room.'

'And she was there?'

'Of course she was there – fast asleep.'

'What time was that?'

She thought for a moment. 'Around two in the morning it must have been.'

Wycliffe fended off a large mongrel dog which had lolloped into the room and wanted to lick his face. 'She has a car, hasn't she?'

'Stop it, Ben! He's terribly affectionate . . . No, the car is ours but she uses it more than we do.'

'Did she go off in it this morning?'

'No, she couldn't have done. Ricky had a bit of an accident last night; he hit the hedge trying to avoid a cat and damaged the steering. It had to be towed to a garage.'

'So she must have been walking.'

'Unless she used her bike; she does sometimes when her father has the car.'

Wycliffe asked to see the girl's bedroom and was taken to a room at the back of the bungalow furnished as a bed-sitter. Everything for the room of a teen-aged daughter straight out of the pages of *Good House-keeping*. It was all there including the record player, the transistor radio and the posters on the wall. What more could a girl want? Yet Wycliffe had the impression that these things were now no more than leftovers and that the room was merely a place to sleep.

'I'm afraid I haven't got round to tidying up – as you see, Margaret is not particular about her clothes.' As she spoke she was picking up from the floor the white jumper and black pants the girl had worn the previous night. The bed was unmade and her pyjamas, too, were lying in a little heap on the floor.

'You don't think anything has happened to her?' Tears glistened in her blue eyes and trickled down her freckled cheeks as she fitted the pants on to a hanger. 'I couldn't bear that; she's all we've got. I couldn't have any more, you see.'

'I shouldn't worry, Mrs Haynes. It's just that we're anxious to talk to her. After all, what could happen in broad daylight?'

She made a consciously brave effort to smile. 'No, I suppose I'm silly; but it's natural for a mother to worry, isn't it? Ricky gets annoyed with me, but it's different for men.'

Wycliffe asked her if she knew what clothes her daughter had been wearing and after she had searched in the wardrobe and a chest of drawers she decided on a blue knitted woollen dress, a brown mackintosh with gilt buttons, and brown, wet-look shoes with block heels and stub toes.

'I can't think where she's gone! I've telephoned round to all her friends . . .' She looked out of the window at the sodden grass and the rather gloomy background of trees. 'Such dreadful weather too!'

'Did she receive a telephone call last night? – after she came home?'

Mrs Haynes shook her head.

'Nor this morning, before she left?'

'No; I would have heard it ring.'

'Could she have made a call without you hearing? Say, this morning while you were in the kitchen getting the breakfast?'

Mrs Haynes hesitated. 'I suppose she could. From the kitchen you can hear the phone ring but you can't hear anybody speaking.'

Before he left Wycliffe confirmed that Margaret Haynes had taken her bicycle.

The girl was a complication he could well have done without. If she was off on some stunt of her own that was no more than a nuisance, but if . . . But why should anyone want to harm her? What had put the idea in his mind?

'I want this girl found.'

They were meeting in the largest compartment of his caravan, his 'operations room' as the press called it. There were ten of them tightly packed around the long table being briefed by Chief Inspector Gill with Wycliffe looking on.

'The last we know of her, she left her home between eight and nine this morning.' He passed round a photograph. 'One like that is being copied and will be circulated. Margaret Dorothy Haynes. Aged 19. Height: 5 feet 6 inches. Weight: 115 pounds. Red hair, blue eyes, freckled complexion . . .'

When Gill had finished, Wycliffe looked round the group at the faces trying to look earnest. 'Any questions?'

A sergeant from Division, mistakenly anxious to be noticed, risked a question. 'Is there any special reason for starting a search so soon, sir? I mean, in the normal way . . .' He broke off, silenced by the blank stare which Wycliffe turned on him. There was a moment while everybody wondered what was coming. Wycliffe shuffled the papers in front of him. 'If she's dead, it's too late.'

Afterwards he had a call from Clement Morley. What did Wycliffe think about Margaret Haynes' disappearance? Surely it must be a coincidence that she had decided to go off? He had heard that George Bryce had been charged with being an accomplice and he hoped that the criminal would not be allowed to slip through the fingers of the police.

Wycliffe said that he hoped so too.

A little later Bellings rang to say much the same thing and got the same reply.

'Bloody fools!' Wycliffe smoked moodily. Jimmy Gill sat opposite him in his little office. As usual the chief inspector was trying to work things out.

'In one way, the fact that she hasn't got a car should make it easier.'

Wycliffe took no notice; he was following his own train of thought. 'I want you to start chatting up the locals, Jimmy. Get all the gossip you can on the Bryce family over the past twenty years; the same for Clement Morley and the dead woman. Why did Morley move to this part of the world in the first place? What is the local version of his sex life? In what circumstances did Matthew marry Caroline? I know that she was pregnant but I want details. How long had they known each other? Was there someone else on the horizon?' Wycliffe broke off. 'You don't look enthusiastic.'

Gill rubbed his bristly chin. 'Surely our first job is to find the girl; we can write their biographies afterwards.'

Wycliffe made a gesture of impatience. 'We've got a small army looking for the girl, Jimmy; you've just briefed 'em. It's our job to keep the case moving.'

Gill got up, seeming to unroll his lean, ungainly length. 'You're the boss!'

Wycliffe's expression was bland. 'That's right.'

'Just one question: do you think Sidney is kinky?'

'Why do you ask?'

'The books on adolescent girls.'

'You mean, if we searched the place, would we find a drawer full of brassières and briefs? Perhaps, but I doubt it. Probably Sidney sees Zel as the daughter he never had. He may have fantasies about her, but he's fond of her and wants to understand her better. The only way he can think of is to buy some books. It's logical, even sensible, I suppose. No doubt a Freudian psychologist would turn it into a phantasmagoria of eroticism, but he might do the same for you or me.'

Gill's sardonic grin almost split his face in two. 'You surprise me, sir!'

'I'm glad. Now get out and let me get on with some work.'

The pile of typescript on his desk had reached alarming dimensions; he had to skim through it on the off-chance that, buried in the pages of inanity, there might be a reply to a question, a casual observation which meant something. If there was he would probably miss it. At six o'clock he switched on the transistor radio and listened to the news. After a lengthy report on the transfer of certain footballers came an item on his murder. 'The murder of Mrs Caroline Bryce, sister of Mr Clement Morley, former Minister of State and prominent front-bencher, continues to baffle the police. The arrest of George Bryce, the dead woman's brother-in-law, is not thought to have brought the case any nearer solution.' Small earthquake in Chile. Few dead. Anti-news. He went across to the hotel for dinner. A stiff breeze blew up the estuary driving fine, cold rain before it. Rain by the sea is so much wetter; the very landscape seems to deliquesce. The fair had not bothered to open but there were lights on in the caravans and appetizing smells came from them. The wharf was deserted but for a couple of sea-gulls perched on the rail, heads to the wind.

He ate without relish and afterwards drank a glass of rum to put some warmth into him for the walk back. He wondered if he was hatching a cold.

When he arrived back at the caravan Jimmy Gill was waiting for him in the main office. Jimmy's chair was tilted back and he had his feet on the table. The duty constable typed conscientiously, eyeing the chief inspector from time to time and wishing that he would put his feet up somewhere else. When Wycliffe came in Jimmy carefully retrieved his feet and righted his chair.

'Anything new?'

Gill followed him into his private office. 'About the girl – Margaret Haynes – somebody saw her going in the direction of George's place on Thursday night, the night Caroline was murdered.'

'At what time?'

'A few minutes after ten.'

'Reliable witness?'

'I think so. He's a railwayman, works at the station, stationmaster, booking clerk, porter – Pooh-Bah of the whole works. He was on two till ten and he was walking back along the tracks to the town. She was walking on the tracks too – the other way.'

'He knew her?'

Gill nodded. 'Apparently she uses the track regularly as a short cut; George does it too when he walks. They're not supposed to, of course, but the railway blokes turn a blind eye.'

'Did he speak to her?'

'Said "Goodnight!" She answered him normally as far as he could tell.'

Wycliffe got out his pipe and started to fill it. The rain was driving against the window now – the wind must have backed a few points – and it was impossible to see anything through the curtain of water streaming down the glass. 'If she was going to Foundry House she would have got there about the same time as Caroline.'

Gill sat himself on one of the folding chairs, riding it. 'She must have gone there. Where else could she have been going?' He reached over and crushed the butt of his cheroot in Wycliffe's ashtray. 'Franks says Caroline was killed by a blow, not necessarily powerful but delivered with a heavy weapon. We've got the weapon and a woman could have used it.'

Wycliffe made an irritable movement. 'You're as full of red herrings as a kipper factory, Jimmy!'

'I'm only saying it's a possibility. After all she and Caroline were after the same man.'

Wycliffe grunted. 'It's possible that she *saw* the murderer.'

Gill whistled. 'And now she's missing!'

Wycliffe said nothing.

Gill waited but when nothing came he went on, 'There's another report. A postman saw the Haynes girl cycling down the hill to town between quarter and half-past eight this morning and the vicar saw her in Station Road a few minutes later.'

Wycliffe was going through the papers in his tray. 'Nothing since?'

'No.' Gill waited then added, 'Station Road is on the way to Boslow and Foundry House.'

'And to the station.' Wycliffe looked up and caught the flicker of a smile on Gill's lips.

'She didn't catch a train; we've checked.'

'Nor the ferry?'

'Nor the ferry.' Gill liked to do his thinking aloud, preferably to an audience; Wycliffe kept his thoughts to himself. Whenever they were alone Gill tried to start a discussion and Wycliffe to block it. It was a game in which both knew the rules.

'On Thursday night she was seen walking along the railway in the direction of Foundry House; this morning she is seen cycling along Foundry Road . . .'

'What about boy-friends? She's only been with

Bryce about six months. There must have been somebody before that.'

Jimmy grinned. 'Half the eligible males in the town.
She's a warm-hearted dolly it seems.' He ran the nail
of his little finger between two of his front teeth and
examined the fragment of food he managed to extract
with approval.

Wycliffe watched him, fascinated. 'You have the
most revolting habits, Jimmy.'

'A man of the people, that's me! As I was saying,
since she left school she seems to have had most
of the boys in the town chasing after her and a
fair proportion probably homed on target. But there
doesn't seem to be much in it from our point of view
– no heart-broken, jealous calf wanting to save her
from herself.' Jimmy Gill had the knack of making the
most human and laudable ambitions sound like the
pipe-dreams of an idiot. 'As far as the lads go, it seems
to have been a brief chase, a quick tumble and "ta ta,
Dolly"!'

'Perhaps that's why she turned to George.'

'Could be, poor little bitch.'

Wycliffe continued to go through his papers. 'I see
you sent a man to talk to the sister – Melinda Bryce.
Any good?'

Gill shook his head. 'Tabb went there. Apparently
she walked out on the family at eighteen and married
a merchant seaman. He did very well for himself and
now he's the skipper of one of the big tankers.' Gill's
expressive hands sketched in the air a tremendous
bulk.

'What about her?'

'Tabb says she seems a very decent sort; inclined to
have a quiet laugh at the family but not malicious –
nor very informative.'

'I imagine it depends on what she is asked.'

Wycliffe worked on his papers for another hour; then he went to the hotel bar and spent the rest of the evening there.

He drank more than was good for him and when he went up to bed his head felt too big for his skull. Before undressing he opened the french window and went out on to the balcony. It had stopped raining, the sky was speckled with stars and away to the south-east he could see every now and then the beam of the lighthouse sweeping out a sector of the sky.

His sleep was disturbed, shot through by vivid, senseless dreams in one of which he was being tried by an Assize Court with Bellings on the Bench. Bellings was saying to him, 'My dear Charles, I charge *you* with being an accessory . . .'

He woke at last, surprised to find the room full of sunshine. The air was chilly, washed clean and tangy with the smell of fresh fish. The sky was blue with billowing white clouds sailing across it. He felt better. Not that he had reached any conclusion about the case – only about himself: he had decided that he was trying too hard. Not far from the window a fishing vessel was unloading her catch with gulls screaming, swooping, soaring and getting very little out of it. He could sympathize.

He felt almost in a holiday mood. What should he do? The answer was to get away somewhere, away from reports, away from Jimmy Gill and, most of all, away from the end of a telephone. All these, at a certain stage of a case, had an inhibiting effect on him. In the Midlands city where he had made his name as a detective he might, when he needed to get away, spend a couple of hours wandering round the covered market or he might sit in a park watching the mothers out with their children, or just walk in the streets.

He called at the caravans. No news of the missing girl. Constable Edwards, a red-faced country youth, was cooking breakfast, boiled eggs for himself and the sergeant.

'Put in a couple for me.' He had not waited for breakfast at the hotel and it was still short of eight o'clock. He ate his two eggs with wedges of brown bread spread with butter and thought that he had never tasted anything more delicious.

Constable Edwards was the sort to flourish in a desert. 'The farmer looks after us . . . none of your shop stuff.'

Two cups of strong tea and he was ready to go. 'Tell Mr Gill that I've been in.'

'Where can Mr Gill get in touch with you, sir?'

The blank stare he received from the chief superintendent reminded him of the tip he had been given: 'Never ask him where he is going.'

He followed the wharf upstream, past the various Bryce enterprises, the boatyard, the cannery, the coal-yard and the timber-yard. It seemed much longer than three days since he had first taken this walk. Was he making for Foundry House or for Boslow? Neither: he was just walking and it was a pleasant day. Without thinking he found himself walking on the railway track, adjusting his stride to the distance between the sleepers. He reached the point where the road doubled back to the town, past the gates of Boslow, but he continued along the track. His mind was almost blank but it occurred to him that Margaret Haynes had walked the same path on the night Caroline had been murdered. The railwayman had not, apparently, been asked whether he had seen her before or after Boslow turn. Gill had assumed that she was on her way to Foundry House but it was possible . . . Thought for the day: Why should she go to Boslow?

He had the estate on his left now, its boundary marked by the bank and by the fringe of trees. Plenty of places where a bicycle and a body could lay hidden. Presumably Jimmy Gill's men had searched; but their search could hardly have been more than cursory. If the girl did not turn up today they would have to get more men on it.

At one point there was a break in the almost continuous line of the bank and a single granite slab, crusted with moss, spanned the stream and led into the woodland. The stream must carry the overflow from the lake and, somewhere, find its way under the railway and out into the river. Wycliffe crossed the bridge and entered the wood. There was plenty of evidence of the passage of heavy feet through the undergrowth, crossing and re-crossing; they had made a thorough search here at any rate. He ploughed through in his turn, traversed the narrow strip of woodland and came out on to a paved area by the lake. The stone slabs of the paving were moss-covered; brambles, springing from between the slabs, formed a tangled web on the surface and here and there gave rise to bushes bearing large, succulent blackberries – the best, he thought, that he had ever tasted.

The lake was larger than he had supposed, and a little way from the shore a sculptured monstrosity formed a small artificial island with granite steps leading up to a group of frolicsome boys and bemused dolphins, inseparable companions in such situations. Away to the right, set back a little from the lake, there was a classical summer-house, its façade pock-marked by peeling stucco. It was only as he went towards it that he saw a punt across the lake with two men in it, previously hidden by the island. Several more men stood in a group on the shore and a police truck was parked nearby. He thought he could spot Jimmy Gill. They were going to drag the lake, and he sat on the steps of the summer-house to watch.

He had scarcely settled himself when he heard a movement from inside the summer-house followed by a stifled cough. He took no notice but continued to watch the activities of Jimmy Gill's team. It was nine-thirty.

At ten-thirty he was still there, immovable as the petrified youths on their island perch. He held his pipe between his teeth but it had long since gone out. There was a sudden movement behind him and Zel came out of the summer-house. She appeared to be surprised to find him there and he pretended to equal astonishment. She had forgotten to button her blouse down the front and exposed her midriff. 'Do you want something?'

He shook his head. 'No.'

Her gaze was on the far side of the lake. 'They've searched the copse; now they're going to drag the lake.'

He noticed that her jeans had little triangular rents in the material showing white skin underneath. 'Won't you sit down?'

She seemed about to refuse, but changed her mind and sat on the step beside him.

'You look as though you've been doing some searching on your own account.'

She glanced down at her jeans. 'I know the place better than they do.' She had glimpsed her unbuttoned blouse and was trying, unobtrusively, to button it.

'But you found nothing?'

'No.'

Across the lake the shore party were paying out rope to the men in the punt.

'Do you know Margaret Haynes?'

'Of course.'

'Well?'

'She was no particular friend.' Her manner towards him had changed since their last meeting. She was no longer indifferent, but antagonistic, perhaps nervous.

'She can't be more than a few months older than you.'

'Six months, actually.' She picked at loose threads in her torn jeans. 'You speak of her as though she were alive, but you know that she is dead, don't you?'

'I know nothing of the kind, there is not a scrap of evidence . . .'

She gestured impatiently. 'It's obvious!'

He got out his pouch and started to fill his pipe. 'You mustn't let your imagination run away with you. Does she ever come here – to the house?'

'Not often. Mother always insisted on me having a stupid party at Christmas and on my birthday; she only did it because she knew how much I hated it. "You should mix more," she used to say.'

'And Margaret came to your parties?'

'Always until this year.'

'And why not this year?'

'I think that she had other things to do.' Her poise was unnerving.

'What sort of girl was she?'

'You know the sort of girl she was.' She was staring

out over the lake, her eyes a little wide, her hands clasped round her knees.

'Men?'

She nodded.

'You know that your Uncle George has been arrested?'

She nodded.

'As an accessory; that does not mean that he killed your mother . . .'

'I know what it means.'

'Tell me what happened on Thursday evening, the evening your mother left.'

'I've told you.'

'Tell me again.' He had only a vague idea in questioning her; had he been completely honest he would have had to admit that he wanted to strike some spark of emotion from her, to disturb her poise.

She repeated her story without hesitation and when she came to the part where she saw her mother leaving, carrying the suitcase, he interrupted. 'Now, tell me *exactly* what happened from then on – She crossed the yard and . . .'

She looked at him, frowning, like a child reciting a lesson anxious to get it right. 'She opened the little back-door of the garage – the one where we keep the Mini . . .'

'Did she have to unlock the door?'

'There is no lock. She went in . . .'

'Did she shut the door behind her? Could you hear her? Did she have difficulty opening the big double doors?' He forced her to tell every detail and she did so without faltering until it came to a question of whether or not her mother had closed the big doors after taking the car out of the garage.

'Listen! You heard her open the big doors, then

there was a short interval while she came back into the garage and got into the car. Do you remember hearing the car door slam?'

'Yes, I think so.'

'Only once?'

'Yes.'

'Then you heard the car engine start and she drove out of the garage?'

'Yes.'

'Right! She drove out of the garage; now, did she stop, get out, come back and shut the big doors or did she drive straight off?'

'She drove straight off.'

'So that the doors were open in the morning?'

For some reason the question disturbed her. 'I don't know; you're confusing me. I don't see that it matters anyway.'

He was dissatisfied. What she had told him did not ring true to his practised ear. Years of listening to prevarication, half-truths and downright lies had given him the perception of a connoisseur where truth was concerned. But why should she lie? Only, presumably, to protect her father. But had she knowledge or mere suspicion?

'I must get back to the house.' She stood up.

'How are your Aunt Joyce and Uncle Francis?'

She looked down at him in surprise, perhaps because of the abrupt change of subject, perhaps because of his familiar use of family names. 'They've gone. Father told them they had to go last night and they left this morning.'

Which meant that there had been a row.

'I'd better get back . . .' Either she wanted or expected him to come with her, but he merely looked at her with a bland smile and nodded.

'I'll go then.'

He watched her stroll with exaggerated nonchalance along the edge of the lake without once looking back.

If she was lying, Caroline could have been killed before she left Boslow, then she could have been driven to Foundry House and the car, with the body in it, left in the boathouse for George to find. The only thing against this reading of the facts was that George said he had found her in the driver's seat. Could it be that Caroline had been murdered by her husband and that he had deliberately set out to incriminate his brother?

The police truck was cruising slowly beside the lake and seemed to be towing the shoreward end of the drag line. Trust Jimmy Gill to think up something complicated!

'You'd better come out now.' Wycliffe seemed to be talking to himself. He continued, 'I'm getting tired of sitting here and you must be tired of being holed up in there.'

There was a movement in the summer-house and after a moment a youth came out, blinking in the sunlight and brushing dust from the seat of his trousers. He was the boy of the self-portrait in Zel's room: the finely-drawn, almost feminine features were unmistakable.

'Sit down and tell me about it.'

'About what?'

'First of all, who you are.'

The boy sat on the step nervously, as though poised to run.

'What is your name?'

'Evans, sir; John Evans.'

'Evans?' The name troubled Wycliffe: he thought he had heard it before in connection with the case.

Then he remembered. 'You're the boy with the motor bike.'

Evans flushed but said nothing.

'Are you still at school?'

'No sir, I'm an apprentice in the boatyard.'

'You like the work?'

'Oh yes; I want to be a designer.'

'But you're not working today?'

'I'm having my fortnight's holiday.'

'You are a friend of Zel?'

'Yes.'

'In love with her?'

He flushed like a shy girl. 'Yes.'

'You meet in there?' He jerked a thumb in the direction of the summer-house.

'Sometimes.'

'On the night of the murder?'

'I was there but she didn't come; she was not well.'

'You left your bike in Station Road – why?'

He shrugged. 'It seemed safer; in any case you can't bring a motor bike along the railway track.'

'Why try to keep your relationship with Zel a secret?'

He hesitated, trying to find words which would not offend. 'It's Zel's people: they wouldn't approve – they would expect her to find somebody better.'

'Her mother knew.'

He seemed genuinely surprised. 'She did? Zel didn't tell me.'

'In any case, good boat-designers make a lot of money.'

He brightened. 'Yes, some do!' But gloom returned. 'It's not as simple as that.' His fists clenched in response to some inner frustration.

'Zel is a very attractive girl.'

'Yes.' The boy gazed across the lake, dully.

'I have a daughter not much older.'

'Oh?' A not very successful attempt to seem interested.

'I think I have a snap of her here.' Wycliffe got out his wallet and handed the boy a coloured snapshot of his twin son and daughter. He handed it wrong side up and the boy took it clumsily, turning it over.

'They're twins.'

'Very nice.'

Wycliffe took back the photograph and replaced it in his wallet.

'I'd better be going: my mother will be expecting me. I promised to do some shopping.' He stood up, hesitated, then made off.

Wycliffe felt restless. At the back of his mind he had the germ of an idea. He could not say exactly when it had occurred to him; perhaps it had been already there when he had talked about filling in the family backgrounds of Morley and the Bryces. He needed to talk to someone who knew them well but could be objective about them. A remark of Jimmy Gill's recurred to him: 'She is inclined to have a quiet laugh at the family – not malicious . . .' Melinda Bryce. If he was right there wouldn't be much to laugh at, but perhaps she would be able to answer some of the questions he wanted to ask. Gill had said that she lived on the other side, above East Treen.

The ferry was at the slipway, silent and deserted. He went aboard and sat on one of the slatted seats, smoking his pipe, for almost half an hour. The pace of life appealed to him: from where he sat he could see nothing that moved but the clouds and the water. Then a furniture pantechnicon came slowly along the wharf and nosed down the slipway. The driver, unaccustomed to such hazards, edged his van gingerly into position, switched off his engine and climbed down from his cab with an air of modest triumph. His arrival seemed to be a signal, for almost at once the two crew members turned up from nowhere, the engine was started, the shoreward gates closed and they were away.

Treen's other half had quite a different character: the hill rose even more steeply and the level ground by the water was scarcely wider than a single street. The houses were in terraces and their little gardens clung to the slope. There were fewer shops and the whole aspect of the place was less prosperous; one had the impression that it had lost any reason for its existence fifty years ago and carried on with a dwindling momentum. It was very warm for late September. Wycliffe looked at his watch but it had only just gone a quarter to twelve. Too early for a drink. One day our permissive society will really get the bit between its teeth and allow a man to have a drink when he feels like one, though we may have to shoot a few brewers and publicans first.

'Zion House?'

An old man sitting on a seat outside the pub directed him. 'Up the hill and the first turning on your left beyond the houses. Just a lane it is – leads to the old mine.'

The pantechnicon passed him and started the long uphill grind to wherever it was going. There was a *Marie Celeste* atmosphere about the place, as though everybody had abruptly evacuated the place for no discernible reason. The houses straggled for a quarter-of-a-mile up the hill then gave way to fields. Wycliffe found the lane, a stony, rutted track between high hedges. Some way ahead a jagged finger of masonry, the broken chimney of the mine, jutted skywards.

Zion House was two-storeyed, square and built of lichen-covered stone roofed with delabole slate and it stood in a walled garden laid out with shrubs and borders which must have required hours of devoted care. A gravelled path led to the front door which stood open. He rang the bell without result so he tried again. A little girl of four or five came round the corner of the house and stood staring at him with solemn black eyes.

'Will you tell Mummy I'm here?'

No answer; but after a further inspection the little girl went off the way she had come and returned a few moments later with her mother. It was only then that Wycliffe realized that he did not know Melinda Bryce's married name.

8

'Trelease.' She peeled off a pair of gardening gloves to shake hands.

Melinda Trelease, née Bryce, was the sort of woman Wycliffe admired: frank, open features, a ready smile and a manner with men which was not sexless but said neither 'Come aboard' nor 'Lay off'. She was dark, as all the Bryces seemed to be, and she had her share of good looks, but what impressed him most was her obvious vitality.

'You've come to ask me about Caroline, I suppose. I've had one of your men here already.' She led him into a large, comfortable sitting-room with a bow window which faced down the estuary towards the sea.

'John, my husband, is a merchant navy skipper – he's away nine months of the year; my son, Philip, is at University and I see very little of him even in the vacations. Young people seem to be very busy these days. So Judy and I have to keep each other company.'

The little girl sat on the settee beside her mother, never taking her eyes off Wycliffe.

'I've not been very intimately mixed up with the family since I was married at eighteen, so I doubt if I can tell you much that you don't know already.'

Wycliffe noticed a rack of pipes by the fireplace and, subconsciously, his hand went to his pocket.

'Do smoke if you want to.'

'Your father disapproved of your marriage?'

She laughed. 'And cut me off without a shilling –

no, it wasn't as bad as that. I didn't fit in at home and marrying John was just symptomatic. Father was old-fashioned in his ideas, but it wasn't that either. It was just that they all seemed to be obsessed with the firm. From infancy I was brought up with the idea that the world would come to an end if the firm had a bad year. It was like a religion with them.'

'Even with George?'

'George was only fourteen when I left home so he didn't really count. Everything one said or did, every friend one made and every quarrel one had was scrupulously and ponderously examined to decide what effect it might have on our business relations. It was ludicrous – mad!' Although she obviously meant what she said, she spoke without heat and certainly without malice. 'Father was a bit of an autocrat, but I wouldn't have held that against him if he hadn't always used the threat of cutting us out of the business. To him it was a fate worse than excommunication – and Matt and Sidney went along with him. I don't blame them, but I just couldn't! And Father couldn't understand a Bryce who thought of the firm merely as a way of earning a living.' She brushed a wisp of hair back from her forehead. 'Luckily I met John, we married and the problem as far as I was concerned was solved.' She smiled at him and put her hand over the little girl's. 'No regrets!'

'You broke off all connection with your family?'

She seemed surprised. 'Good heavens, no! Nothing so dramatic. I visited regularly and I still do, but I've always refused to get *involved*, that's all.'

'Even to the extent of refusing your legacy?'

'That was no great sacrifice. John and I have never been short.'

'Your father died two years after your marriage?'

'In nineteen-fifty-three, yes.'

'And your brother married Caroline Morley shortly afterwards.'

She frowned. 'You're suggesting that there was a connection – yes, I think there was. I don't say that Father stopped the boys from meeting girls or anything of that sort, but he was so damned possessive . . .' She hesitated as though at a loss for words. 'I know it sounds silly but he so filled their lives that they never seemed to have time for anything else.' She grinned, ruefully. 'God defend me from ever doing that to one of mine!'

Wycliffe took time to get his pipe drawing nicely. It was astonishing the extent to which the room expressed the personality of the woman of the house. Its serenity was almost tangible. Trelease must begrudge every day he spent on his oil tanker. She was watching him with a faint smile as though she guessed his thoughts.

'You have been to Boslow and seen what it is like?'

He nodded. 'Your brother Matt's marriage was sudden. Had he known his future wife long?'

'A few months. Clement Morley bought a house in West Treen just before my father died – not the one he has now but a smaller place out towards the headland. Caroline, of course, was his half-sister and she used to come down to stay with him. She was the sort of girl to get herself talked about and she got Morley talked about too for a while. I think she came to Boslow with him two or three times, but when Matt said that he was going to marry her everybody was astounded. Of course, when it turned out that she was pregnant, people thought they understood.'

'Thought?'

She frowned. 'I ought to tell you that I disliked Caroline, so I'm bound to be prejudiced.'

'But?'

She grinned. 'I thought at the time that Matt had been caught, and I've had no reason to think otherwise since. Matt wasn't the sort to sweep a young girl off her feet: he wouldn't have known how to begin. His shyness and nervousness with women were a standing joke. The alternative is to suppose that she made a dead set at him – but why? A man twenty years older, set in his ways, timid and gauche with women . . . I know a girl will sometimes fall for the handsome-mature-man-greying-at-the-temples, but Matt was no film star even in those days.'

'You think that she saw him as a suitable father for someone else's child?'

'I think it's possible. She was the daughter of old Morley's second marriage and he made no secret of the fact that she couldn't expect much under his will. Matthew could give her money and a certain position and Boslow provided a pretty good base for operations.'

'You certainly didn't like her!'

'I told you.'

He stood up and walked round the room with the freedom of an old friend. There were two good pictures and several prints on the walls. One of the pictures was a Fragonard, a saucy boudoir scene.

'Do you like it? Matt gave it me. It used to hang in the drawing-room at Boslow, but nobody appre- ciates painting there and I loved it so much that I overcame my scruples . . .' She laughed. 'John thinks it might give our visitors the wrong idea.'

'You are on good terms with Matt?'

'Why not?'

Wycliffe went to the window and stared out. From this angle the two headlands at the entrance to the estuary presented a 'V' with the sea between. To say that he was thinking would have been too precise a description of the vague notions which were passing through his mind. 'Do you think that Matthew knew or suspected that he had been cheated?'

'I'm certain that he did not.'

'And does not?' He turned to face her.

For the first time she was put out by a question. 'I don't know.'

'If he discovered that Zel was not his daughter . . .'

'But how could he unless Caroline told him; and why should she do that after all these years?'

'Spite?'

She shook her head. 'But Matt would never . . . There's not a scrap of violence in his nature; he is the most gentle creature alive.' However she was disturbed. 'Judy, go and see what's happened to Trotsky.' She turned to Wycliffe 'Trotsky is our cat – a Russian blue as you probably guessed.'

She stood up and brushed the hair from her forehead as though she would rid herself of a tangle of thoughts at the same time. 'I suppose anybody might be provoked; but whoever killed Caroline tried to involve George – isn't that right?'

'It seems so.'

Her face cleared. 'Then you can put Matt right out of your mind! A fit of anger is one thing, but a calculated scheme to shift the blame . . . I'm his sister, Mr Wycliffe, and I know that Matt would be totally incapable of doing such a thing.'

They were both standing now; the serenity of the room was broken. 'Matthew had good reason to dislike his younger brother.'

She made a gesture of impatience. 'He sent him packing from Boslow, but he gave him Foundry House to live in. Is that the action of a vindictive man?' She looked at Wycliffe's face, now a mask of professional reserve. 'I can see that I'm wasting my time; but you will find out for yourself.' She smiled suddenly. 'For God's sake let's sit down; this is absurd! 'Would you like a drink?'

'Very much.'

'Sherry, gin, beer – and I believe I could find a little whisky . . . ?'

'Beer, please.'

She went to fetch it.

If Matthew was not Zel's father, who was? A question which Melinda avoided. Of course it could have been someone who had long since faded from the scene.

She came in with a tray and glasses, an unopened bottle of beer, a bottle of gin and some orange juice. 'Help yourself.' She poured herself a small gin, flushed it with orange and sipped. He poured his beer and took an unmannerly gulp.

'I needed that!'

'Good!'

'What do you think of Zel?'

She placed her glass on the tray. 'I'm sorry for her. She's a strange child – and no wonder, the way she has been brought up.'

'She seems to get plenty of affection from her father and from her uncle.'

'Sidney? Bless his heart! He used to buy books to find out how she should be brought up! They say some women want children without a husband; poor Sidney certainly wanted children without a wife!'

'Do you see much of Zel?'

'Very little. I've tried. Several times recently I've asked her up here – pressed her to come, but she never has.' She frowned. 'I thought I might have helped her. To find her feet in the world a girl needs a woman behind her. Caroline couldn't be bothered so she was left to the well-meaning bumbling of Matt and Sidney.' She brushed a wisp of hair from her eyes and patted it back in place. 'It's a pity she can't find a boy-friend.'

'She has. I was talking to him this morning.' Wycliffe told her of the encounter by the summer-house.

'Evans? I know the boy. I can understand them wanting to keep it quiet. Matt and Sidney would go through the roof.'

'Is there something wrong with the boy?'

'Not that I know of. It's his mother: she has quite a reputation in the town. She's a widow who never seems to have had a husband, and with no obvious means of support.'

Judy came in carrying her rather elegant cat. Her chubby little hands gripped him under the armpits allowing his heavy body to dangle unbecomingly. 'I found him. He was asleep on the water tank.'

Poor Trotsky!

'Why did Matthew throw George out?'

Melinda's brown eyes met his. 'According to Matthew it was because of his affair with Caroline.'

'You believe that?'

She shook her head.

'George says that Matthew accused him of trying to seduce Zel.'

'That sounds a more likely reason.'

'George says that Zel made it up, that she pursued him.'

She shrugged. 'I could believe that.'

'On evidence?'

'Zel is an odd child.'

'She is no longer a child.'

'No.'

Wycliffe looked at his watch. 'I must be off: I'm stopping you from getting your lunch.'

'It won't take much getting and if you care to stay you'll be very welcome.'

He was under the spell of the golden light and the personality of this woman. She seemed to have mastered the difficult art of being female without being either aggressive or coy. They had lunch in the dining-room with french windows open on to the garden. Cold beef and salad with tomatoes, basil and chives with a hint of lemon and garlic; apple pie and cream to follow.

'If you are right about Zel, have you thought who her real father might be?'

'I've thought, of course, but not to much purpose.'

She saw him to the gate and stood with Judy clutching her hand to watch him make his way along the lane until he was out of sight.

Matthew Bryce must have led a lonely, introspective life, trying to recapture with pathetic enthusiasm a time that had passed, trying to preserve methods and traditions of the steam age in the world of the computer and the shop-steward. In his emotional life he had made a late bid for romance and had landed himself with Caroline. But Zel was his consolation, his daughter, that mysterious, alluring enigma – a girl. She was his, the more so in that her mother was antagonistic towards her. Caroline had intrigued with his brother under his roof and he had reacted mildly. Caroline had carried on her affair outside and he had not reacted at all. Events and his relatives were conspiring to take his business away from him but he could take refuge with his models, his prints and his books. He still had Zel.

But what if after eighteen years Caroline had decided to disillusion him? Would he have believed her? Could she have given proof? What sort of proof? Had she named Zel's real father?

'. . . a calculated scheme to shift the blame . . . I *know* that Matt would be incapable of such a thing!' But suppose Caroline had told him that George was Zel's father? When Caroline was eighteen, George would have been sixteen; it was not impossible.

He was back on the water-front, waiting for the ferry, watched by the same old man sitting outside the pub.

'She won't be over for a bit; they'm gone to their dinners.'

He walked by the river towards the sea and his thoughts depressed him. The road soon gave way to a footpath and he found himself skirting fields of stubble, separated from the estuary only by gorse bushes growing on the edge of a low cliff. Such a walk should have restored his good humour, but not now. He sat on a stile, brooding, until he saw the ferry leave the other side; then he walked back to the slipway.

On the way across he stood by the hunch-back. Both of them leaned on the gates, smoking.

'So they ain't found t'other.'

'T'other?'

Dicky took his pipe from his mouth and regarded him. 'The Haynes girl: they bin searching for her over to Boslow all the morning.' He pointed with his pipe-stem to the water swirling past. 'I reckon she'll be turning up one of these days like t'other. They'm wasting their time if you ask me.'

At least they were doing something. What the hell had he been doing? Strolling round like a summer tourist and lunching with an attractive woman.

Dicky spat a brown bolus into the water. 'A nasty business whichever way you look at it!'

True.

Wycliffe walked rapidly and abstractedly along the wharf back to his caravan and did not notice three or four pressmen lolling against the railings until they called to him.

'Anything new, Mr Wycliffe? Why did you have the lake dragged? Do you think the girl has been murdered? Do you expect . . . ?'

'Why don't you boys go home?' As well ask the lions to stop eating Christians.

He pushed open the door of his caravan. 'Is Mr Gill back?'

'Not yet, sir. I think they've moved upstream to Foundry House.'

'Any message?'

'Mr Bellings wants you to telephone him . . .'

Wycliffe handed the sergeant the photograph of the twins which he had shown to the boy, John Evans. 'Handle it carefully and see that it goes at once to Fingerprints.'

Afterwards he continued walking upstream, past the cannary, the coal-yard and the timber-yard, familiar ground now. Beyond Boslow turn he came upon a constable wearing thigh boots and standing guard over a pile of implements and three pairs of shoes with socks pushed in them. 'What goes on?'

'Mr Gill and Constable Edwards are searching the bed of the stream, sir. It's the overflow from the lake and it enters the river, after passing under the railway, further down. The rest of the search party are covering the area round Foundry House, sir.'

Standing on the edge of the bank Wycliffe could see Jimmy Gill and the constable about a hundred yards downstream. Their heads did not reach the level of the banks.

'What size are your boots?'

'Nines, sir.'

Wycliffe took eights but they fitted reasonably: a little long in the legs, but he turned the tops down. When he was comfortable he slid down the steep bank into the stream and started to pick his way after the others. The bottom was gravel without any boulders and the water scarcely came over his ankles except where the stream had scooped out miniature whirl-pools. It would be a different story after a few hours' rain. It was a strangely different world between the steep, fern-covered banks; the air was saturated with moisture and with the acrid smell of sodden earth and rotting vegetation. A fish shot away from his feet and a cloud of gnats maintained station round his head.

The other two were taking their time and he soon caught them up. Gill greeted him with a cynical smile. 'As you see, sir, we are leaving no stone unturned.'

Wycliffe did not answer.

'We dragged the lake this morning.'

'I know.' Wycliffe stumbled as one foot went into a pool which was deeper than most. Gill grabbed him. 'Hey up! At least it's quiet down here – far from the madding crowd and all that. It could catch on as a new sport – stream-walking.'

'For God's sake don't tell the BBC. They'll have an outside broadcast team on it before you can blink.'

They covered another hundred yards and the stream

turned to the left and into a culvert under the railway. Arched over with granite blocks it was high enough to stand up in. The old Great Western never skimped or botched a job.

'This is where the stream goes through to the river.'

'So I had imagined.'

As they entered the culvert, Jimmy Gill, who was leading, stopped them. 'We've found her.'

A moment for his eyes to become accustomed to the gloom and Wycliffe could see the figure of a girl lying in the stream, one leg doubled beneath her. She was wearing a brown raincoat with gilt buttons, and now the wet-look shoes with their block heels were really wet. Beyond he could see the gleaming chromium of her bicycle.

At that moment they were startled by a sound like approaching thunder and it was overhead before any of them realized that it was a train of waggons on the way to West Treen. Wycliffe waited for the rumbling to pass, then turned to the constable. 'Get out where you can use your personal radio, tell them the news and ask them to get busy. I would like Dr Franks to join me here as soon as he can.'

When he had gone Jimmy Gill shone his pocket torch on to the girl's head. She was lying face down in the water, her red hair streaming forward in the gentle current. The base of her skull was a mass of hair and clotted blood. 'Not such a clean job this time,' Gill said. 'I reckon he must have had two or three goes.'

Wycliffe was silent.

'She was last seen on Thursday morning, cycling along Station Road. It's now Friday afternoon.' Gill made his calculation. 'She can't have been here more than thirty hours.'

'So?'

'I don't know. Most of yesterday it was pissing down with rain; I was wondering whether there could have been enough water in the stream to carry her down from further up.'

'And her bike? No, somebody slung the bike in and dragged her in after it.' Wycliffe was still gazing down at the girl's body. 'Let's get out of here!'

They walked a little way upstream and climbed the bank. The sunshine was an indecency and Wycliffe could not help thinking of his own daughter who was near enough to the same age as the dead girl in the culvert.

Jimmy Gill lit a cheroot and puffed vigorously, as though the acrid smoke was a breath of fresh cleansing air. 'It begins to look bad for your friend Matthew.'

'He's no friend of mine, but I find it difficult to see him as a murderer. All the same . . .'

'If he killed his wife he must have done it before driving her over to Foundry House; and Zel saw or heard enough to know what had happened. When he got there he drove the car into the boathouse, transferred the body to the driving seat and strapped it in. It must have been a premeditated crime because she was killed with a piece of lead pipe like the scrap in the corner of the boathouse and he left his weapon there. In any case he must have known that George would be out or he wouldn't have dared.' Gill smoked in silence for a while. 'It fits. The Haynes girl was on her way to see George on Thursday night. She didn't know he wasn't there, or she was prepared to wait until he came back. As she arrived in the clearing she saw Matthew come out of the boathouse. She kept out of the way until he had gone, then she took a look in the boathouse to see what he had been up to . . .'

'Plucky girl!' Wycliffe was satirical.

'All right! Perhaps she didn't go into the boathouse. When she heard that Caroline had been found there she would put two and two together . . .'

'And?'

'Well, one possibility is that she tried a spot of blackmail on Matthew.'

'Are you saying that, yesterday morning, Margaret Haynes went to Boslow, rang the front door-bell, accused Matthew of murdering his wife and was then lured here, killed and pushed into the culvert?'

Gill grinned. 'You've got the knack of making reasonable ideas sound bloody silly if you don't like them.'

'That idea is bloody silly.'

But Gill was not put off. 'All the same, I think we should put the screw on Matthew.'

Wycliffe did not answer and the chief inspector went on: 'What bothers me is the question of motive. I would like to feel that we were on firmer ground there. As you said yourself it's difficult to understand why a man should suddenly murder his wife after putting up with her for nearly twenty years. There must have been a crisis.'

Wycliffe sat on a weathered granite block of which there were several between the railway and the stream, vestiges of some forgotten enterprise. He got out his pipe. 'I had lunch with Melinda Bryce.'

Gill was sour. 'Good for you. I'm still waiting for mine.'

'She thinks Zel is not Matthew's daughter.'

'Then whose?'

'That's a question. But if Melinda is right and if Matthew only recently discovered the fact . . .'

'We have our crisis and our motive ! She could have blurted it out in a row from sheer spite !'

'We still have to prove it,' Wycliffe grunted.

9

The naked body of the girl, once Margaret Haynes, lay face downwards on the dissecting table. Dr Franks, in his white overall and wearing surgical gloves, stood on one side, Wycliffe on the other. Her red hair had been gathered into a top-knot and held by a surgical clip; the base of her skull around the damaged area had been shaved.

Franks, pink and chubby like a healthy baby, was intently examining the girl's feet. 'The fact that she has been lying in running water means that all the post-mortem changes are retarded . . . Also there is a certain amount of rigor remaining . . .'

Wycliffe shifted impatiently. 'Save all that for your students. How long has she been dead?'

Even with twenty years of experience behind him Wycliffe was never at ease in the presence of death. Franks, on the other hand, had acquired a cheerful, cynical indifference and a ghoulish sense of humour which jarred on the detective. The only flaw in a professional relationship which had ripened into friendship. Franks approached a post-mortem with a gusto and relish which might be admirable in a craftsman of another sort.

'You're always in a hurry, Wycliffe; you should relax more – your arteries are probably beginning to tell a tale. Take notice – I do.'

His fingers, short but tapering, like musician's, were running over the limbs as he spoke.

'Thirty to thirty-six hours at a guess, but I may have reason to think again . . .'

'Yesterday morning at eight-thirty she was seen alive near where we found her.'

'Then it looks as though I've hit the jack-pot again.' He bent over the girl's head, probing gently round the damage. 'It seems as though she was hit at least twice and probably three times. One of the blows was more violent than the others and, as you can see, she lost some blood – more than you'd think from the look of this. Some of it was probably washed away.'

'So you think she was put in the stream immediately after receiving the blows?'

'There is some damage to the top of her head and lacerations of the face; these would be consistent with her having been struck down while she was on the bank and falling into the stream. It's a messier job than the other.'

'The same sort of weapon?'

Franks looked at him in mild reproof. 'How the hell do I know until I've made a proper examination? There's no reason why not: the Bryce woman might have been in a more favourable position from the murderer's point of view – bending down, say.'

'Is Caroline Bryce's body still here?'

Franks shook his head. 'The undertaker fetched it away this morning; they're having the funeral tomorrow. The coroner issued a certificate . . .'

'Nobody tells me.'

Franks chuckled. 'Your office has certainly been notified but you're never there to know one way or the other.'

'Cremation?'

'Nope! Burial in the churchyard; all nice and respectable.' He looked at Wycliffe with sudden concern. 'Why? You're not suggesting . . .'

'I suppose you've still got your copies of the photographs?'

Franks was more puzzled. 'What the hell are you getting at? I get a set, but so do you . . .'

'Show me yours, there's a good chap!'

Franks hesitated but gave in. 'OK! I suppose this will keep for another ten minutes.' He motioned to one of his assistants to draw a sheet over the body.

He peeled off his gloves and led the way through a tiled corridor to an office which looked out on to a little garden. He unlocked a filing cabinet and drew out an envelope. 'Here it is. Now, for Christ's sake tell me what you're after!'

The envelope was bulky and contained upwards of thirty full-plate photographs of the dead woman, taken from every angle, with clothes and without. Wycliffe shuffled through them. 'Don't say . . .' He broke off. 'Ah! Here we are.' He held out a photograph of Caroline's head and neck taken in profile; the black hair was drawn back from the eroded features exposing one ear – the left. He pointed to the ear. 'Is that an attached lobe?'

Franks took the picture. 'You can see for yourself.'

'Never mind what I can see. I'm asking you as an expert.'

'Well, of course it's attached – why?'

'Put it in a supplementary report; we may need it.'

'I suppose it's no good asking . . . ?'

'Am I right in thinking that it is impossible for a couple, both with attached ear lobes, to have a child whose lobes are free?'

Franks, like all experts, shied from the categorical

167

reply. 'If we are right about the genetics of the thing – yes. The attached or adherent lobe is inherited as a recessive so that it would be impossible for parents with attached lobes to hand on the dominant, free-lobed condition to their children – why?'

'Because Caroline and Matthew Bryce both have attached lobes and the girl, Zel, has not.'

'Ergo, the girl is a bastard. You do have fun!'

'It may not be so funny as you think.' All the same Wycliffe seemed, suddenly, to be in a better humour. 'Have a good evening. I'm off.'

He drove at his usual sedate pace back to the caravans and arrived there after the sun had set and the whole estuary was filled with purple mist. The water was glassy, lambent and mysterious. He now rated sufficient importance for the hotel to lay on a special meal for him whenever he arrived, but he had no enthusiasm for a tough steak with potatoes and carrots out of tins. WPC Rowse happened to be on duty in the caravan.

'Can you cook?'

'I can do you a bacon and cheese omelette, sir.'

After his meal he telephoned Clement Morley and asked to see him. Morley was reluctant and haggled, but without much conviction. 'It's late and I still have a great deal of work in front of me . . . Yes, I heard about the finding of Margaret Haynes' body, on the News. Very sad; terrible, in fact. I suppose you know that she worked for me part-time doing shorthand and typing . . .'

Wycliffe was silent.

'All the same, I don't see how I can help you.'

'That's for me to judge, sir.'

'Very well, you'd better come along. Say in half-an-hour.' He sounded subdued and worried.

168

Wycliffe parked his car in front of the house as the church clock was counting out the strokes of ten. The weather was on the change and a cold, damp breeze off the sea played tricks with the sound, whisking it away, then tossing it back with startling clarity. The squint-eyed old spinster who should have been a housekeeper in a presbytery showed him to Morley's study without a word. Morley received him with a certain deference. He looked ill; his pallid skin showed a dark flush under the eyes. 'A terrible business, Wycliffe. On top of the other it has quite unnerved me.'

Wycliffe seated himself opposite Morley with the desk between them; the ex-minister matched his bony fingers and studied them. 'I came to know the girl through her father who is the golf "pro". She seemed to be drifting as so many young people do these days and I thought it would be a kindness to offer her a job.'

Wycliffe cut in without ceremony. 'It was not about Margaret Haynes that I wanted to talk to you, Mr Morley. At the moment I am more concerned with Mrs Bryce.'

The brown eyes rested on Wycliffe's for a moment then flitted nervously away. Something had knocked the stuffing out of Clement. 'Caroline? What can I tell you that you don't already know?'

Wycliffe's manner was calm, placid, disquietingly so. He seemed in no hurry to come to the point.

'Would you like a drink?'

'No, thank you.'

'Smoke if you wish.'

'I am going to ask you some questions, Mr Morley, and I should tell you that I am in a position to satisfy myself as to the truth of your answers.'

'That is an insulting remark!' A flash of the old Morley.

But Wycliffe seemed not to hear. 'When you first came to Treen, nineteen years ago, you had a smaller house, near the headland?'

'While I looked round for a more suitable place, yes.'

'Your half-sister came to stay with you?'

Morley had unclasped his hands and he was looking at his upturned palms with curious concentration. 'Once or twice. She took a fancy to Treen as I had done.'

'It was during one of these visits that she met and married her husband?'

'It was.' Morley put his palms together again and rubbed them gently. 'I was invited to Boslow and I took Caroline with me on two or three occasions.'

'Did she seem interested in Matthew or attracted by him?'

Morley hesitated. 'Not especially.'

'So that you were surprised when she said that she intended to marry him?'

'I was more than surprised. Like everyone else, I was astounded!'

'And you did your best to discourage her?'

'I had no influence over Caroline but I pointed out how unsuitable the match would be.'

'You did not know at the time that she was pregnant?'

'I did not!' He raised a hand to his eyes as though to brush away a source of irritation. 'Look here, Wycliffe! I can see no point in raking over the past.' If it was an attempt to recover the initiative it was still-born; it hardly got off the ground.

Wycliffe's bland stare did not waver. 'Very well, let

us come to recent events. When I was here on Tuesday you seemed anxious to know if the police had been through your half-sister's papers and personal effects – why?'

'Surely it is natural that I should want to know whether there was anything that might shed light on her death?' He reached into a cupboard under his desk and brought out a decanter and glasses.

'Would it surprise you to know that there was?'

Morley's hand was unsteady as he poured himself a drink. 'Are you sure that you won't join me?'

'Please answer my question.'

'I don't see how I can unless I know the nature of the . . . the evidence.'

'Do you know that Matthew is not Zel's father?'

Morley's quick, nervous glance had a wild quality like that of a trapped animal. 'Rubbish! Who has been retailing such wicked gossip?' All the same he could sit no longer. He stood up, glass in hand, and moved to the window. The curtains had not been drawn and he stood with his back to Wycliffe, staring out into the darkness. 'Really, Wycliffe!'

But Wycliffe was unmoved. He sat in his chair, seemingly calm and impassive, but his mind was furiously alive. A great many things, including, perhaps, his career, depended on how he played his cards now. 'I have proof that Zel is not Matthew's daughter.'

'Proof! I can't believe it!' Morley's face was invisible but his voice was tremulous and he seemed to have lost control of its pitch.

'Proof that would stand up in court. It was a well-kept secret until last week when Caroline chose to tell her husband.'

A silence which lengthened. It was one of Wycliffe's

less obvious assets that he knew how to endure silence. Few people do. The ticking of Morley's grandfather clock became suddenly audible, then intrusive and, finally, dominant. Morley continued to stand with his back to the room, motionless. The ticking of the clock imposed a rhythm on the silence, adding to the tension. An aeroplane throbbed in the distance, came nearer, then its sound died away.

Morley turned. He looked composed but he groped for his chair like a blind man and sat down.

Wycliffe spoke. 'You have not asked me who her father is.'

Morley made a tiny gesture of helplessness. 'You know?'

'Yes.'

The ex-minister seemed to have aged; his cheeks sagged and he was suddenly thinner, poorer. 'It would have finished me.'

Wycliffe's gaze was unfocused; he might have been absorbed in his private thoughts or half asleep.

'All my life I have hated certain things . . . I have fought against them – *fought*!'

Wycliffe had a sudden, vivid memory of a group of boys exchanging dirty stories behind the lavatories in the school yard and of one boy, standing apart, his ears cocked, trying to catch the forbidden words.

'I'm not a hypocrite; I've really believed in what I've tried to do.'

Three days ago Wycliffe had come near to hating this man, his pomposity, his offensive patronage, his assumption that he was entitled to special treatment. He would have anticipated with satisfaction the chance to deflate him, to expose him as a fraud. But not now.

'I was twenty-eight, she was eighteen. I had seen very little of her since leaving home six or seven years earlier. She was almost a stranger.' He smoothed his blotting pad with the palm of his hand. 'She was lovely. I could not think of her as a relative . . . she seemed a different kind of being.' He looked away, across the room. 'I had never had a woman . . .'

Wycliffe waited.

'Even so I would never have . . . She teased me, taunted me for the way I lived, laughed at my . . . my restraint . . . It was only the once, just the one time.

'Then, after a while, she told me that she was pregnant. I had no experience; I was green. But I knew enough to know that with money these things could be put right. It was simply a question of making the right contacts. Believe me, I had a struggle with my conscience, but the alternative was unthinkable . . . I had just been elected to Parliament and already I had begun to establish some reputation as one who stood for the old values of decency and reticence . . . and here I was with my half-sister!

'But she would not hear of an abortion. For weeks she kept me in an agony of suspense then, one morning at breakfast, she said, "Clem, your troubles are over – for the moment." I thought that her . . . that she meant the whole thing had been a mistake on her part but, after a little while, she added, "I'm going to marry Matt Bryce; he thinks it's his." She seemed to look on the whole thing as a huge joke. "We are going to get married in a Registry Office so that it won't look too bad." What could I do?'

With the absurd deliberation of a man who is either drunk or undergoing great mental stress, Morley arranged the items on his desk, placing them with such care that his life might have depended on their symmetry.

'As the years went by I came to believe that it had

all worked out for the best. Although Caroline was now living in Treen I saw very little of her and when we did meet there was never any reference to what there was between us. I heard talk of her affair with George Bryce but Matt did not seem to mind and it was none of my business although I suffered indirectly through being related to her. Then, five years ago, when my father died, there was a change. Caroline and my other half-sister, Joyce, did not get what they thought they were entitled to, and Caroline blamed me.'

'She blackmailed you.'

Morley stroked his cheeks with his fingers then looked at his hand uneasily as though he expected something to have rubbed off. 'It wasn't blackmail. I made her certain regular payments.'

'Quite large sums.'

'The payments were made openly, by cheque. There was nothing underhand on my side.'

'But she threatened you.'

He would not meet Wycliffe's eyes. 'From time to time she reminded me of what was rarely out of my mind and pointed out how damaging it would be if people got to know . . .'

There was silence again except for the ticking of the clock. Once more Wycliffe forced Morley to break it. His voice sounded harsh and unnatural. 'I did not kill her.'

Wycliffe did not even look at him.

'Why should I want to kill her? I could afford to pay what she asked and, in a way, it helped to . . . to . . .'

'To ease your conscience?'

'Yes.'

Wycliffe got out his pipe and started to fill it. The

position was so different now; almost, it seemed that Morley would need to ask the detective's permission before he poured himself another drink or lit a cigarette. The human peck-order is far more subtle than that of the hen-house.

'I didn't kill her.'

'Perhaps your half-sister decided that she was no longer satisfied with money.' Wycliffe spoke between puffs at his pipe, causing the flame of the match to undulate over the bowl. 'It is possible that, being a vindictive woman, she might get more satisfaction from exposing you.'

Morley gestured helplessly. 'I can't *prove* anything, but I tell you I didn't kill her!'

Wycliffe did not answer directly. 'Evidently Margaret Haynes knew too much and she had to be silenced.'

'You can't think . . .'

Wycliffe stood up.

'You're going?'

'I'll find my own way out.'

'But . . .'

'You were going to say?'

'Nothing.'

Wycliffe was at the door and he did not turn back. Morley followed him into the hall but he was too late: the front door slammed.

It had started to rain, just a fine drizzle, and as Wycliffe drove back to the town the street lamps were haloed.

Next morning Wycliffe went to the funeral. It was fine, with a blue sky and powder-puff clouds, but the air was moist, threatening rain. There were more people about than usual, perhaps because it was

Saturday and the women were doing their week-end shopping. In the square there were stalls around the war memorial, selling fruit and vegetables, cheap clothing, hardware and second-hand ornaments. Women gossiped in little groups and Wycliffe thought that they eyed him with some hostility as he passed. He was not surprised. One murder in a small town is exciting, something new to talk about. Two are a different matter; people begin to feel that somebody has slipped up, their security is threatened and they naturally hold it against those who are there to protect them.

Wycliffe joined the funeral party in the church. Family and close friends occupied the front pews; then there was a large gap separating them from a score or so townspeople who sat at the back. Wycliffe took a position in no-man's-land.

The family was there in force, all except George. Matthew wore an ancient black suit which was too big for him; Sidney was immaculate in clerical grey. Zel was between them, wearing a bottle-green winter coat with fur trimmings; she sat bolt upright, staring in front of her. Joyce and Francis Boon were in the front pew on the other side of the aisle. Joyce had a chic, black two-piece while Francis wore a dark overcoat probably hiding something wildly unsuitable underneath. He looked unnaturally pale and stared round the church as though trying to remember why he was there. Clement Morley sat next to Francis and kept turning towards him as though irritated by something he was doing. Melinda Trelease sat with Cousin Irene behind the brothers; she must have found somebody to look after Judy. The church was heavy with the rather oppressive scent of the flowers heaped on the coffin and disposed round the altar.

They filed into the churchyard. Like most of Treen it was on a steep slope and the bearers had to carry the coffin up a path broken at intervals by short flights of steps. The old part of the churchyard was sheltered by pines but the new part had only recently been taken in from the surrounding fields and Caroline's grave was dug through rough grass. Wycliffe had expected a family vault. As they gathered at the graveside, Morley caught his eye and looked quickly away. He was still very pale with dark rings under his eyes. Zel, too, was pale; she stood at the edge of the grave as they lowered the coffin into it but never once looked down, Matthew, on the other hand, never took his eyes off it. It was impossible to divine his thoughts; almost certainly he was looking back over nineteen years during which there must have been some moments of happiness. Joyce Boon held a little handkerchief and dabbed her eyes; Cousin Irene, in black from head to foot, wept unashamedly.

'Forasmuch as it has pleased Almighty God in his great mercy to take unto himself the soul of our dear sister here departed, we therefore commit her body to the ground . . .'

Gulls suddenly screamed overhead in a running dog-fight, drowning the voice of the priest. Wycliffe was aware of little groups of sight-seers dotted about the churchyard. What did they expect to see? An avenging spirit rise from the grave of the murdered woman?

At last it was over and they trooped down the hill with the vicar holding Zel's arm and speaking soothing words. At the gate she deserted the vicar abruptly and came over to Wycliffe. She was secretive and intense. 'I must talk to you, it's urgent!'

The car for the chief mourners drew level and

stopped. Matthew and Sidney stood to one side, waiting for Zel.

'I shall be at Boslow later today.'

This did not satisfy her and she would have argued, but Joyce Boon, with Francis in tow, stopped to speak to the chief superintendent. 'It was good of you to come; the family appreciate it very much.' She seemed to be a self-constituted master of ceremonies but her eyes were red. Perhaps she had really been weeping for her sister. Zel got into the car reluctantly and was driven away.

Clement Morley made a point of not seeing Wycliffe; he was picked up by his own car, the black Mercedes with a chauffeur at the wheel. Wycliffe walked back through the town to the water-front and to his headquarters. Chief Inspector Gill was waiting for him.

'Good funeral?'

Wycliffe went through into his office and sat down. Gill followed him. 'Are you going to see Matthew?'

Wycliffe nodded. He was thinking about Caroline, about the funeral and the motives which had drawn the family together in this strangely moving ritual centred on a dead woman who was certainly not loved by most of them.

Gill took up his favourite position, astride one of the chairs. 'What's all this about ear lobes? I don't get it.' He had been reading some notes Wycliffe had dictated for the record.

Outside the estuary was grey, swept by a sudden shower. Saturday morning. Nine days ago Caroline Bryce was still alive. What had happened in the last ten or twelve hours of her life? It seemed to Wycliffe that he had made remarkably little effort to find out; he had been content to nibble round the edges.

Meanwhile Margaret Haynes had also died. Last Saturday at this time she still had four days to go . . .

He recollected himself and realized that Jimmy Gill was watching him with a malicious grin deepening the lines of his ugly, intriguing features. 'Ear lobes.'

Wycliffe gathered his wits. 'It's a question of inheritance. A couple whose ear lobes are attached cannot have a child with free lobes. Matthew and Caroline both have attached lobes and Zel's are free.'

'So we have proof?'

'Yes.'

'But no proof that she is Morley's.'

'Only his admission.'

Gill rubbed his bristly chin. 'I don't see why he should have admitted it. He has everything to lose.'

'Morley thought that Caroline had left some evidence that he was Zel's father and when I told him I had proof that Matt was not, he assumed the worst.'

'Self-incrimination by a trick.' Gill was facetious.

'Morley isn't accused of any crime.'

'That's right, he isn't – not yet.'

Wycliffe detested Gill's probing. He hated having to explain himself, not because he was modest but because he was ashamed of the vagueness of his mental processes. Some of his colleagues were only too anxious to expose the rational processes by which they had reached certain (correct) conclusions but Wycliffe had never indulged himself. Often after he had arrived at some decision he found himself trying to rationalize it to satisfy others. Gill might well ask, 'What made you pick on Morley as the girl's father?' He hardly knew himself. To start with he remembered looking at Zel and thinking, 'There's very little Bryce in you.' Then he had heard that Morley had made regular payments to his half-sister and somebody,

George probably, had said that Caroline 'had something on Morley'. And only the previous morning Melinda Bryce had told him that Caroline had been the sort of girl to get herself talked about and 'for a while she got Morley talked about too'. It was only afterwards that he had seen the possible significance of the remark. But, perhaps, the idea had first been seeded while he was looking at the photograph of Morley's mother which hung in his study. He had been struck by her thick lips which she had handed on to her son. Zel had them too, in less degree. It was only the previous afternoon while he was talking to Dr Franks in his dissecting room that the obvious had occurred to him: *Morley's mother was not Caroline's.* How then could Zel . . . ? So a fact here, a fact there, collected in the rag-bag of his memory would suddenly fall into a pattern. But how could such a random and fortuitous process be explained?

'I'm going to lunch.'

Just as he was leaving a telephone message came for him.

'The prints on the photograph you sent us include a fresh set which match those on the steering wheel of the vehicle abandoned . . .'

'What the hell is all this?' Gill demanded.

'He's Zel's boy-friend and I think it very likely that he drove the car with Caroline's body in it from the Boslow garage to Foundry House.'

'You mean the girl got him to do it in order to save her father?'

'How should I know?' Wycliffe was suddenly ill-tempered. He gave instructions for Evans to be brought in.

Wycliffe lunched at the hotel, where there were more people than he had yet seen. Farmers who had brought their wives Saturday-shopping came to the hotel for lunch. It was a regular feature of the off-season life of the little town; everyone seemed to be on first name terms with everyone else and the manager spoke of them collectively as his 'Saturday Regulars'. Despite the heavy and frequent showers the fair had started early and its canned music blared insistently creating a holiday atmosphere.

The superintendent came in for a lot of surreptitious attention; people pointed him out and whispered. One man who had spent too long at the bar explained loudly to his embarrassed companions why the Area CID was bound to be less efficient than the Yard.

After lunch he went back to his headquarters. In the big room of his caravan Constable Edwards was typing reports while John Evans sat opposite, across the table. Sitting by Evans was Matthew Bryce. They sat there, the boy and the man, looking for all the world as though they were waiting for the dentist. Wycliffe greeted Bryce curtly and ignored the boy. He went through to his own office and Constable Edwards followed him.

'What's Bryce doing here?'

'He arrived about half an hour ago, sir. He wants to see you and he insisted on waiting. I couldn't get out of him what it's about.'

'Have they spoken to each other – Bryce and the boy?'

'Not a word, sir.'

Bryce probably had not the least idea why Evans was there. Evans would certainly know Bryce and he must be very worried, wondering why he was there with Zel's father and how much Wycliffe knew. No wonder he was white and tense.

'Send him in.'

'My Bryce, sir?'

'The boy.' Wycliffe got out his pipe. 'Bryce can wait if he wants to.'

'He's soaked to the skin; he must have walked from Boslow and he hasn't even got a raincoat . . .'

Wycliffe paused in the act of lighting his pipe. 'The boy! And take Bryce over to the other van; I don't want him eavesdropping.'

'These partitions are almost sound-proof, sir.'

'Do as I say!' Occasionally Wycliffe indulged himself in a fit of deliberate bad temper, deriving a certain satisfaction from the concern and discomfort he created around him. He had the wit to realize that these fits came when he was least sure of himself and they helped to restore his self-confidence.

John Evans came in and stood nervous and gangling near the door of the little office, looking at Wycliffe.

'Sit down. How long have you been waiting?'

'About an hour, sir.'

Wycliffe stared at him with a gloomy expression. 'Good! I hope it was long enough to make you decide to tell the truth.'

The boy flushed. He sat nervously on the edge of one of the collapsible chairs pulling his fingers so that occasionally a joint cracked.

'Don't do that!'

'Sorry.'

They sat in silence while Wycliffe turned the pages of a report.

'How old are you?'

'Eighteen and a half, sir.'

'A responsible adult!' Wycliffe raised his eyes from the report and looked at him. 'Can you drive a car as well as a motor bike?' The boy hesitated. 'It's a simple matter to find out.'

'Yes, I can drive a car.'

'Good! Now, I'm going to caution you, then I shall ask you to tell me what you did on the night Mrs Bryce was murdered – last Thursday week.'

The pale blue eyes flitted round the room as though seeking escape. 'I don't know what you mean.' But the denial was only half-hearted.

'Your fingerprints were on the steering wheel of Mrs Bryce's Mini and your motor bike was seen, parked at the end of Station Road, after eleven o'clock on that night.'

'Oh God!' The words, little more than a sigh, were also a surrender.

'Zel came for you, didn't she?'

'Yes.'

'Tell me about it.'

'I go to art class on Thursday nights and I had just got back. I got off the bike and I was going to push it into the court where we live when I saw her coming down the street.'

'What did she say?'

He licked his lips. 'She was very upset; she said something had happened to her mother and she wanted me to come back with her. I took her on the pillion and we drove to Boslow. She made me stop at the end of Station Road.'

'Then?'

'We went in the back way and in to the garage where they keep the Mini . . .' He broke off and Wycliffe waited for him to go on. 'Zel's mother was lying there on the floor between the car and the double doors of the garage. She was dead.' His gaze was fixed on the ground as though he could still see the dead woman lying there.

'What did you do?'

'I was afraid . . .'

'Of what?'

He moistened his lips. 'I could see that she had been . . . that she had been killed.'

'And you were afraid that Zel had done it?'

He nodded. 'I asked her and she told me not to be a fool. She wanted me to help her to get . . . to get the body to her uncle's house. At first I wouldn't do it but she . . .' He broke off and hid his face in his hands. When he looked up his eyes were full of tears.

'She told you that if you refused to help her to save her father from arrest you couldn't really love her and that it would be all over between you. Is that it?' Wycliffe reeled off the words as though repeating a formula and they had a curiously bracing effect on the boy.

'She told you?'

Wycliffe said nothing.

'Anyway I did what she wanted. We got the body into the passenger seat of the car and I drove it to Foundry House. We put the car in the boathouse and shifted the body to the driving seat and strapped it in.' He shuddered. 'It was horrible!'

'Then?'

'We walked back to Boslow. I hardly knew what I was doing. I tried to persuade Zel to go to the police.

I think I threatened to go myself.'

'But you didn't.'

He shook his head, miserably.

'From the time you drove away from Boslow until you got back, did you see anyone?'

'No.'

'Think!'

'We saw nobody; it was late . . .'

'Did you know Margaret Haynes?'

'Yes.'

'Well?'

'Well enough to speak to her if we met in the street.'

'Have you ever had intercourse with her?'

The boy flushed. 'No.'

'Apparently she went with a number of young men?'

'So they say.'

'You know that she has been murdered too?'

'Yes.'

'We think she was killed because she knew something about Mrs Bryce's death. Now, are you quite certain that you did not see her that night?'

The boy's eyes were riveted to the chief superintendent's. 'Certain.'

'One more question, equally important. Between the Thursday on which Mrs Bryce died and the following Thursday when Margaret Haynes disappeared, did she make any contact with you?'

'No.'

'With Zel?'

'Not as far as I know, and I think Zel would have told me if she had.'

Gill came in and stood in the doorway, sizing up the situation. Wycliffe nodded. 'This is John Evans; he is going to make a statement.'

The boy looked from Wycliffe to Gill and back again with fresh apprehension.

'Constable Edwards will take your statement next door.'

Evans stood up. 'Are you going . . . Shall I be allowed to go home after . . . ?'

Wycliffe softened and spoke kindly. 'We'll see. I think we'd better find you a lawyer.'

'Poor little bastard!' Gill said when the boy had gone. 'That's what comes of listening to a woman!'

Wycliffe was looking out of the window of the caravan. The rain had stopped again and there was a pale, golden light over the estuary as the sun struggled through. Gill took his usual seat on one of the collapsible chairs.

'It looks bad for Matthew. The girl must think he did it – or she must know that he did.' He lit one of his cheroots. 'I suppose the next move is to Boslow?'

'No need: Bryce is here, in the other van, waiting.'

'You sent for him?'

'He came of his own accord.'

'To give himself up?'

'How should I know? You'd better bring him over.'

When he came in, Bryce looked frail and ill. There were dark patches of damp on his shoulders and sleeves and on the knees of his trousers.

'I thought I'd wait until after the funeral.' He sat on one of the chairs, his hands resting listlessly in his lap.

'Before doing what?'

He looked up in surprise. 'Giving myself up. I thought you understood.'

Wycliffe's expression was utterly blank. 'No.'

'I killed my wife.'

'And Margaret Haynes?' The question came sharply from Gill.

Bryce nodded.

'You wish to make a statement?'

Bryce stirred like a man required to make an effort beyond his strength. 'If that is what I have to do.'

'I must caution you . . .'

'Do you mind if I smoke?' He took out a packet of cigarettes which were crushed and damp.

They moved to the larger room and Wycliffe sent for WPC Rowse to take shorthand. The interrogation began. Wycliffe and Gill sat at one side of the long narrow table and Bryce at the other. WPC Rowse made herself inconspicuous on a chair by the door.

'She told me that she was going to stay with her sister, Joyce . . .'

'Did you believe her?'

Bryce glanced up in reproof. 'Does it matter?' He was so tired that any interruption to his train of thought made it difficult for him to go on. 'I knew that whatever she said she would take the car. She has been disqualified before and it made no difference. I went out to the garage to wait for her. I can't say how long I waited but, at last, I heard her footsteps as she crossed the yard. I had the light on and when she came into the garage she found me going through some nuts and bolts I keep there. She muttered something and passed round on the other side of the car to open the big double doors. I got there first and stooped down, pretending to have trouble with the lower bolt. She was impatient as usual. "Let me do it!" she said. "I'm in a hurry." So I let her take my place and as she bent down I hit her with a piece of lead pipe across the base of the skull.' He paused for a long time. 'She collapsed without a sound; I couldn't believe that it was all over.'

The room was full of smoke. Bryce was taking short, deep inhalations from his cigarette. Gill had his cheroot going and Wycliffe gripped his unlit pipe between his teeth. Gill was watching Bryce with ferocious intensity. 'How did you intend to dispose of the body?'

Bryce noticed the accumulated ash on his cigarette and knocked it off in the common ashtray. 'I hadn't any clear idea . . .'

'You must have thought about it.'

Bryce shook his head. 'I don't think so. I couldn't see beyond the actual . . .' He hesitated for a word.

'Killing – is that what you are trying to say?'

'I suppose so, yes.' He seemed dissatisfied and after a moment added, 'I don't think that I expected to avoid the consequence of what I had done. After a while I went indoors, to my room. I didn't go to bed that night.'

'And next day?'

'Next day I put off going into the garage and when I did, I thought I must be losing my reason. The body was gone and so was the car! For a moment I wondered if it had all been a dream. Had I really murdered Caroline?'

Wycliffe watched Jimmy Gill grind out the stub of his cheroot. 'Did it occur to you that you might not have killed her, that she might have got up and driven away?'

He shuddered. 'Good God, no! There was no question of that!'

The vigour of his denial surprised Wycliffe.

'All right, go on.'

The gaze of his good eye wandered vaguely over the

table-top never lifting to the eyes of his questioners. 'You can imagine the state in which I spent the next days, not knowing what had happened to her body . . . When, on Tuesday, it was taken from the estuary, I was in no better shape.' He stopped to light a fresh cigarette from the butt of the old. The afternoon sun was streaming in through the windows and it seemed that the rain had gone for good. Bryce blinked in the sunlight.

'Would you like the curtains drawn?'

'What? No, I'm all right. I was saying, on Tuesday they found her body and in the afternoon you came. Then, on Thursday, I heard that her car . . . that George was mixed up in it. It was unbelievable!' He stopped speaking, as though living again in his mind the events of which he told. 'That morning I met the girl, Margaret Haynes . . .'

'By arrangement?'

'What? No, certainly not. By chance. I was out for my morning walk and I met her on the far side of the lake near the summer-house. She seemed to want to speak to me . . .'

'You knew her?'

'Of course! She had stayed at the house several times for Zel's parties.'

'Do you take a walk every morning?'

'I rarely miss.'

'Always the same walk?'

'I suppose so – yes.'

'So that Margaret Haynes might have counted on meeting you there?'

Bryce looked surprised as though the idea was new to him. 'Yes, I suppose she might; I hadn't thought of that.'

Gill was doing the questioning now, Wycliffe

seemed to have lost interest. He had started to fill his pipe and appeared to be absorbed in his own thoughts.

'Anyway, what did she say to you?'

'She asked me if I knew who had killed my wife and I said that I did not. I wondered what she was after and thought it might be something George had put her up to. Then the shock came. She told me that she was at Foundry House on the night Caroline died and that she had seen Caroline's Mini driven into the boathouse. A few minutes later Zel and a boy had come out . . .' Bryce's voice faltered and he broke off.

'You believed her?'

'Of course I believed her! Why should she make up such a story? In any case it explained what had happened.' He focused his good eye on Gill. 'It also meant that Zel was in grave danger; that was the thought uppermost in my mind. You must believe that. I asked her whether she had told anyone what she had seen and she said that she had not. I didn't stop to think, to reason out a course of action. It seemed to me then that I had no other course. I struck her across the base of the skull with the heavy ash stick which I carry when I am walking and the poor girl went down like a log.' He shifted his position in his chair and his right hand smoothed the table-top as though to remove unseen irregularities.

'You hit her only once?'

'I don't know. It is possible that I did more. For a few moments I must have been insane.'

'It is important.'

His good eye wavered in its gaze. 'I can't be sure. As I said, I think I was mad.'

'What did you do then?'

'Do?'

Wycliffe stirred himself. 'You had a body on your

hands; did you just leave it there in the hope that somebody would come along and dispose of it for you a second time?'

Gill looked at Wycliffe, surprised by the irony. Bryce seemed not to notice. 'No, it was broad daylight so I had to do something. I carried her into the undergrowth and hid her as well as I could; then I hid the bicycle – she had been wheeling a bicycle – in the same way.'

'She was not found in the undergrowth.'

'I know. That night I went out and . . .'

'Why did you kill your wife?' Wycliffe cut in across his words and surprised even the WPC who looked up from her book to see what was happening.

'I . . .' Bryce made a helpless gesture and was silent. Wycliffe smoked placidly. Gill, obviously puzzled by the line Wycliffe was taking, chose to keep quiet. The WPC studied her shorthand notes. Wycliffe's bland state never left Bryce's face.

'Was it because she had told you that Zel was not your daughter?'

Bryce winced as though from a blow. For a moment he said nothing; then, in a voice that was scarcely audible he murmured, 'So you know.'

Wycliffe was still watching him. Not a muscle of the chief superintendent's face moved. The silence lengthened. When it seemed that it might never end, Bryce went on in a more controlled voice. 'She knew that Zel was the only human being in the world I cared for, and she had to destroy . . . to destroy the legitimate basis for that affection.'

'You were having a row?'

He nodded. 'During supper that night, Zel went up to her room . . .'

'You believed what your wife told you?'

He was staring at his hands, spread out on the table-top. 'She made sure of that; she told me to ask Morley.' He turned to Gill as though seeking support. 'Can you believe that a woman . . . ?'

But Wycliffe, utterly impassive, interrupted him again. 'So you killed her to keep the truth from Zel?'

He shook his head. 'No, I had no right to keep the truth from Zel. I killed her because she was not fit to live.'

Abruptly, Wycliffe stood up. 'All right, Mr Bryce. Your statement will be typed and then, if you wish, you may sign it.' His brisk, almost cheerful manner seemed out of place. Gill was puzzled.

'And after I've signed?' Bryce stood up, wearily.

'One thing at a time.' He called a constable. 'Take Mr Bryce to the other van and stay with him until his statement has been typed; then let him read it and sign it.'

Bryce went out, followed by the constable. Wycliffe watched him cross the grass to the other caravan; his tread was heavy. WPC Rowse uncovered the typewriter. Gill followed Wycliffe into his private office and sat down. 'So that's that, then?'

'You think so?'

Gill grimaced. 'I suppose it makes sense. I couldn't really believe that the old boy killed the Haynes girl to protect himself. But to save Zel – that's a horse of a different colour.'

'But he hasn't saved her.'

'No.'

Wycliffe was looking out of the window. The ferry was grinding its way across to the east bank, apparently empty. Bryce kills his wife, Zel and her boy-friend thoughtfully plant the body on his brother who disposes of it for them. Bryce then murders the girl, Margaret Haynes, because she saw something of the part Zel played in the business. Wycliffe shook his head.

Gill, for once, was watching him in silence. 'When he's signed his statement you'll have him charged?'

Wycliffe did not answer.

It was almost six when they told him that Bryce had signed his statement. He crossed the grass with Gill at his heels to the other van. Bryce was still seated at the table with his signed statement in front of him. His signature, in a bold flourish, would have looked more in keeping at the foot of a painstakingly engrossed Victorian lease.

Wycliffe picked up the statement, weighing the little wad of typescript in his hand. 'You came here of your own accord, Mr Bryce, and made this statement voluntarily. Are you willing to go on helping us?'

Gill looked at him as though he had taken leave of his senses; even Bryce seemed surprised.

'Aren't you going to charge me?'

'You can't be charged here; we shall take you over to Divisional Headquarters where you may be asked some more questions. I'm sure you will understand that there are several points to be cleared up. Of course, you are entitled to have your solicitor present.'

'No.'

'As you wish.' Wycliffe's manner was kindly but indifferent. Motioning Gill to follow him he went out and they walked a few paces on the wet grass.

'I don't get it!' Gill said.

'I want him stalled and I want you to go to Division with him to make sure they understand the position. He can be questioned, he can make another statement if he wants to, he can see anybody he wishes or he can spend a quiet night in a cell, but he's to be kept out of circulation – helping us with our inquiries.'

Gill was on the point of arguing but changed his mind.

Wycliffe had been tense and ill-at-ease, but when Gill and Bryce were driven off in the police car he seemed to relax. He walked over to his own van and stood in the central office staring out of the window into the early dusk.

'Can I help you, sir?' The duty constable watched him with concern.

Wycliffe turned as though surprised to find that he was not alone. 'What? No.' He filled his pipe and lit it. 'I'm going out.'

'Sir?'

Wycliffe looked at his watch. 'Ring Boslow and ask for Mr Sidney Bryce. Tell him that his brother, Matthew, has been here, that he has made a statement and that he is continuing to help us with our inquiries; he will not be home tonight.'

The constable scribbled rapidly.

'Got that?'

'Anything else, sir?'

'You can tell him, also, that I am on my way to see him.' Wycliffe went into his office and came out wearing a shabby fawn raincoat.

'I'll get you a car, sir.'

'No, I shall walk. You get on with your telephoning.'

He stood on the steps of the caravan in the drizzling rain, his coat collar turned up, his hands deep in the pockets. He set out, following the wharf upstream. The fair was hard at it, the bright lights mistily diffused. The ferry was at the slipway, its navigation lights burning. Wycliffe walked with head bent, a preoccupied, shabbily-dressed, middle-aged man in a hurry.

When he reached the beginning of the railway track he took to it and paced the sleepers with no apparent awareness of his surroundings. He left the line near the entrance to Boslow and walked up the drive between the dripping laurels.

There were no lights showing in the front of the house but when he rang, the door was opened almost at once by Sidney, looking strained and anxious. 'I had just got in when your man telephoned . . .'

Wycliffe became aware for the first time that his mackintosh was wet: it was dripping pools of water onto the floor.

'Let me take your coat . . .' Sidney held the mackintosh at arm's length. 'What sort of statement has Matthew made?'

'A confession.'

'To murder?'

'To the killing of his wife and of Margaret Haynes.'

Sidney was distraught. 'I can't believe it! I must see him – where is he?'

'He is at Divisional Headquarters. I was going to suggest that you go over with Zel.'

'You think that Zel should go?'

'I think so, yes. Where is she?'

Bryce looked embarrassed. 'She's with Cousin Irene – Miss Bates, our housekeeper.'

'Good! I want to see Miss Bates.'

'I hardly think that is possible. Apparently Matt told Irene something of what he intended to do and she's very upset; she's made herself ill.'

'You mean that she's drunk.' There were times when Wycliffe could be brutal.

'The worse for drink, certainly.'

'I still want to see her.'

'I don't think . . .' But Wycliffe was halfway up the stairs.

Irene's room was almost in darkness. Zel came from the direction of the bedroom and whispered: 'She's asleep.' Wycliffe went to the bedroom door, opened it and peered in. The room was very small with a latticed window high in the wall. A brass-railed single bed, a chest of drawers and a fireplace with a gas fire, a bamboo table near the bed with a night-light already burning. The room stank of gin. Wycliffe crept in and stood looking down at Irene. She was breathing heavily and she looked like an old woman. Her dentures were in a glass on the table and without them her lips were pursed together as though in a self-satisfied smile. He went back to her sitting-room closing the bedroom door behind him. Zel was standing by the window looking down into the yard.

'He told her?'

'So it seems. She took it badly.'

'And you?'

She turned to face him; in the near darkness her face was a pale blur. 'I want to talk to you; I wanted to this morning.'

'Is anything wrong?' Sidney was standing in the doorway. His futile question remained unanswered. Wycliffe went and switched on the light. Irene's cat jumped down from its chair, stretched, clawed the carpet, then padded out into the passage.

'I lied to you about what I saw on Thursday evening, the night my mother . . .'

'I know.'

He had never seen her in a dress before; it was of a green, silky material, patterned with black arabesques, and it made her a woman. She sat in one of the easy chairs, pulling her dress down over her long, straight thighs. She was pale with dark areas beneath her eyes.

Sidney hovered nervously. 'I don't think you should say anything to the chief superintendent, Zel . . . It's not that we have anything to hide but I am sure that we should consult . . .'

Wycliffe was standing by the window now, lighting his pipe. Sidney's protest died away and neither of them took the slightest notice.

'Your mother did not leave here alive on Thursday night, did she?'

'Is that what he told you?'

'Is it the truth?'

She nodded. 'Yes.'

Wycliffe puffed at his pipe to get it going. 'Before you say any more I should tell you that I know John Evans drove the car with your mother's body in it to Foundry House. I know also that it was your idea and that you went with him.'

The girl merely murmured, 'I see.' Complete acceptance.

Sidney was scandalized. 'But Wycliffe! You really can't . . . !'

'I must caution you . . .'

She listened to the formula with indifference.

'If all this is true, she did it to protect her father!' Sidney Bryce had interposed himself between Wycliffe and the girl as though to ward off a physical threat.

'Be quiet!' She might have been speaking to a child and Sidney looked at her in astonishment as though he were seeing her for the first time. She had her hands clasped round her knees and she was looking down into her lap as though she were ashamed. 'I want to tell you the truth. Everything happened as I told you up to the point when I saw my mother cross the yard and go into the garage.' She looked up quickly to meet Wycliffe's bland stare. 'I stood by the window. I suppose I was waiting to hear her open the big doors, start the car and drive away; but nothing happened. I waited for what seemed a long time . . . and still nothing. I was puzzled . . .'

'What did you do?'

'I couldn't think what she could be doing in there so I put on my dressing-gown and went downstairs to find out.' She stopped speaking.

'Well?'

'I went out to the garage and I found her lying on the floor between the car and the doors. She was dead. I could see . . . I could see where she had been hit and there was a piece of pipe lying beside her.'

'During the time you were looking out of the window you did not see your father?'

'No.'

'Nor afterwards?'

'No.'

'The main doors of the garage were still shut?'

'Yes.'

'Can they be opened from outside?'

'No: there is a bar across which holds both doors.' She was answering his questions in a low but distinct voice and she seemed composed.

'Go on.'

'I was distracted. I didn't know what to do.'

'You thought that your father had killed her?'

'You shouldn't answer that, Zel!'

She looked at her uncle as though surprised to find him still there, but she answered Wycliffe. 'It seemed the only explanation; they had been having rows.'

'What did you do?'

'I got dressed, then I ran down to John's place. Luckily I caught him just as he was coming back from Evening Class. I got him to come back with me.'

'To do what?'

She pressed her hands between her knees and hunched her shoulders. 'I hardly knew; I couldn't think clearly. All I wanted was to get her away from the house. John wouldn't help at first but I persuaded him . . . We got the body into the car and while we were doing it I thought of George's boathouse. Don't ask me why; I wasn't being logical – it just seemed a good idea . . .'

'You knew that your uncle would not be at home?'

'It wouldn't have mattered if he was; the boathouse is too far from the house. In any case he isn't usually home until very late.'

'So you persuaded John Evans to drive there and you went with him?'

'Of course; he wouldn't have known what to do otherwise. When we got there I made him help to get her body into the driver's seat, then we strapped her in and left.' She paused, staring at the floor for a long time. Wycliffe said nothing and she went on at last, 'You see, I thought she would be found there and they would think she had driven over to see George and somebody had attacked her.'

'You walked back to Boslow?'

'Yes. John was in a terrible state and I wasn't sure he wouldn't go to the police, so we stayed together a good while.'

'What about the piece of pipe?'

'The pipe? Oh, I wanted to get rid of that so I took it with me in the car and dropped it on a pile of scrap in a corner of the boathouse.'

Outside a rising wind blew rain against the

windows. Sidney Bryce stood, shocked and bewildered, not knowing what to say or do.

'You did all this to protect your father?'

'Yes.'

'Then why tell me about it now?'

'Because it's useless now and last night he told me something that changed everything.' She seemed to expect a question but none came.

'Last night he told me that I am not his daughter. He thought that he had better tell me before someone else did.'

'Zel! My poor child!' Sidney's voice was anguished and he moved to the girl's side and put his arm round her protectively. She shook him off.

'Leave me alone, for God's sake!'

Poor Sidney; his world was crumbling. And yet, it seemed, he could be no more than a spectator.

Wycliffe was standing by the window holding his pipe which had gone out. She looked up at him, her voice brittle. 'Do you like riddles? I'm not my father's daughter, so who am I?'

Despite himself he was touched. 'I'm sorry.' The words seemed to have been forced from him.

She was picking at a loose thread in the hem of her dress. 'Sorry? Why? Because I am the result of dirty games between my mother and her half-brother? I expect that sort of thing happens all the time.'

This was too much for Sidney. He confronted Wycliffe. 'Half-brother? Does this mean that Morley . . . ?'

'Is my father – yes, he is,' Zel answered him. She turned to Wycliffe. 'You don't seem surprised.'

Wycliffe's blank stare never faltered. 'I knew.'

'How could you possibly know?'

'It's a long story.'

'Not as long as mine; it took me eighteen years.'

The house was silent. It seemed to be quite dark outside: the window of which the curtains remained undrawn was a rectangle of blackness. Wycliffe was oppressed by a sense of unreality: the girl herself, the events she described, the room with its depressing reminders of a woman who drank herself into a stupor because she was superfluous, and an awareness of other rooms in the house, rooms which were no more than refuges.

'Your father is at our Divisional Headquarters. Do you want to see him?'

'No.'

'I think you should.'

She looked at him and seemed to read something in his expression which made her change her mind. 'All right.'

'Your uncle will take you over.' He turned to Sidney, addressing him directly for the first time since they had come into the room. 'If you prefer it I will send for a police car.'

Sidney seemed to come alive abruptly. 'No, I'll take my own car.'

'I'll wait for you downstairs.' Wycliffe went slowly down the white staircase into the dimly-lit, cavernous hall. At the bottom of the stairs he turned towards Matthew's workroom, opened the door and switched on the light; the musty smell was overpowering. The room had undergone a transformation since the last time he had been in it and it was evident that Matthew had not expected to come back. The shelves had been stripped and the books sorted into heaps, there were large cardboard boxes labelled with lists of their contents and, on the table by the window, there was a large envelope addressed to Sidney and boldly endorsed: 'Instructions for the disposal of my books, models and papers.'

Wycliffe gave all this scant attention. He crossed the room to the french windows. They were secured by a bolt and a spring lock; then he left the room, switched off the light and shut the door behind him.

A minute or two later he was joined in the hall by Zel. 'He's gone to fetch his car.' She was wearing the green coat she had worn to the funeral and carrying a lizard-skin handbag.

'Will Miss Bates be all right on her own?'

'I suppose she'll sleep it off as usual.'

Sidney Bryce brought his car round to the front of the house. He made a great business of locking the front door while they waited on the gravel. Then he got into his car with Zel beside him. 'Can we give you a lift back to town?'

'Thanks, I'll walk.'

The rain had stopped and the rising wind stirred the branches of the elms so that crisp, papery leaves fluttered down like pale moths.

I I

When the tail-lights of Sidney's car had disappeared
he went to the back of the house and let himself in
through the french window to Matthew's room. Once
inside he made for the kitchen. It was a barn of a place
which had not been modernized or even thoroughly
cleaned in thirty years. He looked in the refrigerator,
a monster of white enamelled metal and varnished
wood. It was empty except for the remains of a ham
and a bottle of white wine which had been opened.
He cut himself some ham, found a loaf of bread in the
larder, and ate the ham with dry bread, sitting on a
corner of the kitchen table. Probably because he had
not eaten for several hours, he enjoyed it. He thought
of Bellings and smiled to himself. He considered
making tea or coffee. There was a kettle on the gas
cooker but when he tried to light the ring he found
that the gas had been turned off at the main. He
washed down his food with the white wine, over-
chilled and almost tasteless.

He was in for a long vigil, but the prospect did not
depress him. In earlier days he had kept observation
on countless occasions, often for seven or eight hours
at a stretch and once for seventeen hours without
relief. He rather liked the long periods of enforced
inactivity coupled with the need to remain alert.
One noticed things which normally escaped attention,
sounds, smells, the shapes of buildings, the profile of
roofs. One became aware of subtle rhythms in the

progress of a night and of a unique succession in every dawn. There was time to think.

Sidney Bryce and Zel must have reached Divisional Headquarters. Wycliffe wondered what they had said to each other on the way. Probably very little. Sidney would have made several attempts, but Zel had almost certainly rebuffed him, brusquely, even cruelly. Would her interview with Matthew take place with Sidney looking on? Probably; they would need his presence to guard their tongues. Their only true communication would be through looks, small gestures and words which did not mean what they seemed to say.

He was moving round the house with a freedom which could only come from the certain knowledge that he would not be disturbed. He had plenty of time. He was tempted to light his pipe, but he knew that for the non-smoker fresh tobacco smoke is as salutary as a shout. First he went to Cousin Irene's room. He crept through the sitting-room and in to her almost airless little bedroom. She was still deeply asleep but her breathing was quieter. The yellow light seemed to blanch her features.

Opposite her sitting-room, across the passage, was a linen cupboard. He opened the door and swept the interior with the beam of his pocket torch. There was a kitchen chair, probably used to get linen down from the higher shelves. It might be useful later. He worked his way along the main corridor, looking in all the rooms, and found Matthew's bedroom. It was small and looked over the yard. There was a single bed, a bookcase, a chair and sisal matting on the floor. He opened the window and put his head out; he could smell the sea and hear the music of the fairground carried on the wind.

It was after midnight when he heard Sidney's car. It stopped by the garages at the back and, listening, he could follow the business of putting the car away and shutting the garage doors. He heard footsteps in the yard but no voices; then the back door was unlocked and they were in the kitchen. A moment or two later they came out into the hall, the staircase lights were switched on and Wycliffe retreated down the passage to his linen cupboard.

'He didn't seem too upset.' Sidney's voice.

There was no reply.

'Try not to dwell on it, Zel.'

Still no answer.

'Would you like one of my tablets to help you sleep?'

'No.'

'Goodnight, Zel.'

'Goodnight.'

He heard Zel go up the stairs to her attic and the lights were switched off. The darkness seemed absolute. He sat on his chair with the door of the cupboard open and it was not long before he could make out the foreshortened rectangle of the door and then, beyond it, the gleam of the glass knob on Irene's door across the way. He settled down to wait.

There were vague, indefinable sounds of movement; a lavatory was flushed and for some time after that water gurgled through the plumbing. Then there was silence. As the darkness had seemed absolute at first, so did the silence, but it was not long before the house seemed to be full of sounds, minute crepitations, creaks and even small thuds and squeaks. Rats? More than once he was almost convinced that someone was creeping stealthily down the corridor but nobody passed between him and the dimly reflective knob on

Irene's door. Then something brushed silently against his legs and he barely suppressed an exclamation. Irene's cat. It mewed plaintively then moved off.

He would have given a great deal for a smoke but otherwise he was content. It seemed that the wind had dropped again; probably it was raining. He looked at the luminous dial of his watch: one o'clock. He shifted into a more comfortable position and the chair creaked horribly. His eyes remained fixed on the door across the passage, almost hypnotized by the dull gleam of the glass knob. The knob seemed, suddenly, to change its position; it appeared to be staring down at him like a malevolent eye. He must have lost his sense of orientation in the instant of dozing off and he pulled himself together with a convulsive start. It was then that he caught the first whiff of gas. At first he thought that he had been mistaken; then he smelt it again, insidious and persistent. In a single movement he was across the passage and in Irene's sitting-room. He switched on the light, not caring now. The smell of gas was definitely stronger – the gas-fire in her bedroom! Yet no-one could have got into her room without him seeing. Or could they? He blundered into the bedroom and there the smell was much stronger, though still not overpowering. He could hear the gentle hiss of escaping gas. He stooped, turned off the tap on the fire and the hissing ceased.

He went to the window, struggled with it for a moment, then got it open so that the chilly night air flooded the little box of a room. Cousin Irene stirred and made some inarticulate sound. He went to the bed and hoisted her on to his shoulder, carried her into the next room and lowered her into one of the armchairs, then threw open the big window until the sashes met. When he turned back to Irene she was blinking at him, dazzled by the light. He went back to her bedroom, gathered up an armful of bedding and tucked her up in the chair. Then he extracted an arm from the bundle and took her pulse. It was slow but not, he thought, dangerously so. All the same . . .

He went down the passage, knocked on Sidney's door, opened it and went into his sitting-room.

'What is it?' Sidney stood in the doorway of his bedroom, pulling on a dressing-gown over silk pyjamas. 'Wycliffe! What are you doing here?'

Wycliffe told him what had happened. He was like a man who wonders from what direction the next blow will come.

'Will she . . . ?'

'She'll be all right. I want you to stay with her while I telephone.'

He went downstairs to the telephone and spoke to the duty officer telling him to send the police surgeon and a WPC. 'And let Mr Gill know.'

When he returned to Irene's room she was vomiting into a basin held in Sidney's trembling hands. Zel arrived and stood in the doorway. 'What's happened? What's the matter with her?'

Wycliffe told her. 'The doctor will be here soon.'

'Will she be all right?'

'She'll probably have nothing worse than a hangover in the morning, and she must be used to that.' He turned to Sidney and asked him to fill a hot-water bottle.

'Zel will do that.'

'I need her here.'

Sidney went.

Zel helped him to get Cousin Irene back to bed and to tuck her in. The gas had cleared and they were able to shut the windows.

'She must have tried to kill herself.'

Wycliffe said nothing. Sidney came back with a hot-water bottle. 'She'll be all right now until the doctor comes.'

As they stood by her bed Irene opened her eyes and looked at them. The vacant stare resolved itself into fright and she tried to sit up, shouting, 'No, no, I won't!' Wycliffe was able to calm her and soon she was sleeping again.

'I'll stay with her,' Zel said.

'No, I want to talk to you.' Wycliffe took her arm and led her into her mother's sitting-room. Sidney followed, hesitantly, as though he half expected to be sent away. It was chilly and Wycliffe switched on the electric fire. 'Sit down.'

She sat in one of the low chairs with orange cushions and pulled her dressing-gown over her knees. She looked very young. 'I knew she was upset but I never thought she would try to kill herself.'

'When you came in with your uncle, why did you turn the gas on at the main?'

Sidney was standing behind Zel's chair, his hands gripping the back. 'What are you talking about? I don't understand how you came to be here. Obviously it's fortunate that you were, but I still think you owe us an explanation . . .'

Wycliffe ignored him.

She swept the soft black hair back from her face. 'I turned the gas off; we always turn it off at night.'

'The gas was already off. You turned it on.'

She frowned. 'I see what you're getting at. I suppose it's possible I made a mistake. If it was off already and she'd left her fire turned on . . .'

'My God, Wycliffe, even if that's what happened,

208

you can't blame the poor child for that – not after all she's been through!'

Wycliffe was standing on the hearth-rug, looking down at the girl. He did not even look up at Sidney's interruption. 'It was no mistake. Before you left with your uncle you had turned the gas off at the main and the tap on in Miss Bates' bedroom; then, when you came back, you turned on the main before going to bed.'

'Why should I do that?' She asked the question in a level voice without a trace of emotion or fear.

'Because you wanted to kill Irene Bates.'

'What?' Sidney bleated.

'You were afraid that she was ready to tell me what she had seen from her window on the night your mother was killed. Fortunately, in the morning, she will still be able to do so.'

She was perfectly calm; in fact he noticed that her hands, which had been clenched in her lap, now relaxed.

They heard the drone of a car engine in the distance, then the sound of a car in the drive and the screech of wheels braked on gravel.

'They've arrived,' Wycliffe said.

He was driven to Divisional Headquarters in a police car. Gill sat in front with the driver. Wycliffe and WPC Rowse were in the back with Zel between them. They were expected. An office was put at Wycliffe's disposal and he had arranged to talk to Matthew Bryce before taking the case any further.

He sat with Gill in his office, smoking and waiting. The clock on the wall, with Roman numerals under its fly-blown glass, showed five minutes past three. The internal telephone rang and Gill answered it.

'Is he dead? . . . Have you sent for a doctor?' A longish interval, then, 'You've got good reason to be!' He slammed down the receiver. 'That was Clark, the duty officer. Matthew Bryce has killed himself – slashed his wrists. When they went to fetch him they found him on the floor of his cell – dead.'

'They've got a doctor?'

'Apparently the police surgeon was in the building on a drunk-in-charge case. Bryce is dead all right. Incompetent bastards! Clark says he's worried; I told him, he's got reason to be.'

'Bryce wasn't a prisoner; he was here voluntarily.'

'A fat lot of good that will do us in the bloody press. In any case, you'd think they'd have kept an eye on him. A man doesn't die that way in five minutes.'

They went downstairs to the cells, a short, tiled passage with two cubicles opening off and security doors. On the floor of one of them Matthew Bryce lay in a pool of his own blood. A young man in a raincoat stood by with Inspector Clark, the duty officer. Clark was near retirement, a copper of the old school, with close-cropped hair and a reassuringly massive bulk. 'Chief Detective Superintendent Wycliffe, Dr Oates, our police surgeon.'

Wycliffe looked down at the dead man. 'How long do you think, doctor?'

'Since he did it? Quite a while. At a guess, I should say three or four hours.'

'His brother and his daughter must have been here at eleven. How long since he was last seen?'

Inspector Clark spoke as though he were giving evidence. 'His visitors left at 11.15, sir. He then said that he would like to settle down for the night. A constable got him a glass of hot milk from the canteen and he was brought down here. It was explained to him that he was here of his own accord and that he was not under any form of restraint. The door of the cell was not locked.' The inspector's anxiety to cover himself irritated Wycliffe, but with an inevitable inquiry ahead, who could blame him?

'So your men saw nothing of him from, say, 11.30 until – until when?'

Clark hesitated. 'Until ten minutes ago, sir, when the sergeant went to tell him you wanted to talk to him.'

Wycliffe looked at the dead man. Although he had known him for such a short time he felt a bond of sympathy. He wished that the doctor had closed the eyes. The good one, staring upwards, was more disquieting than the damaged one, which looked much as it had done in life.

'He left this.' The inspector held out a sheet of paper torn from a pocket diary. It must have been found on the floor for it was stained with blood. On it a message written in pencil:

'*I am too much of a coward to face the consequences.*'

'What did he use to cut his wrists?'

'Razor blade, sir. We had no right to search him.'

'Save the excuses, Inspector!' Wycliffe snapped.

'Reasons, sir, not excuses.'

'There was no-one in the other cell?'

'No, these are new. There's a drunk in the old block; that was why we put him in here.'

So Matthew Bryce had not lived long enough to know that his self-sacrifice would go for nothing. Wycliffe turned away. 'Send the girl upstairs to me.'

She came accompanied by a policewoman. She was pale but composed. Her face looked a little thinner, her eyes a little larger; like the rest of them she must be very tired. She glanced at Gill and Wycliffe in turn and took her seat. The policewoman stood by the door.

'I have bad news for you, Zel.'

She gave no sign that she had heard.

'Your father – Matthew Bryce . . .'

'What about him?'

'He has taken his own life; he left this note.'

She took the note, read it, and handed it back with no visible sign of emotion.

Wycliffe waited for her to speak but she said nothing. She had presumably noticed that the paper was stained with blood, but she did not even ask how he had died.

'I'm sorry. If you go with the policewoman she will see that you have a chance to get some sleep.'

'Won't you question me?'

'That can wait.'

'No.'

'You want to make a statement?'

'If that's what you call it.'

Wycliffe cautioned her.

'I killed my mother and Margaret Haynes. I tried to kill Cousin Irene.'

It is strange that more and more of the drama of our lives seems to be played out in dingy offices in front of officials.

'You want to tell me about it?'

'Yes.'

At a sign from Wycliffe the policewoman came to the table and prepared to take notes.

'Why are you so anxious to tell me now? You tried to kill Miss Bates because you thought that she might give you away.'

She shrugged. 'But you found out. I knew that you would, sooner or later; it was only a question of time.'

Gill lit one of his cheroots. 'You expected to be found out?'

'I'm not a fool.'

'Then why . . . ?'

She shifted irritably in her chair. 'I wanted to make them suffer – all of them.'

'All right, go on.'

The institutional cream paint on the walls was peeling in places; the lamp, suspended by a long flex, cast only a small circle of bright light, so that much of the room was in shadow. Outside the streets of the town were silent and deserted; only occasionally a car sounded a long way off, drew nearer, then seemed to rush past the police station. WPC Rowse recorded the girl's statement, her head bent over her book, her blonde hair shining in the light.

'It was Monday when I decided what I would do. We were having supper and they had started to quarrel. I got up and walked out. They must have thought I had gone to my room; but I listened outside the door.'

Wycliffe had the picture in his mind. The gloomy dining-room, the only common ground in the house, no-man's-land. Sidney could not have been there; they would not have quarrelled in front of him. But Irene was there, a nonentity, of no more account than the furniture.

'She was shouting at him, as usual; he said nothing or almost nothing. She was practically screaming with temper. "You've given me nothing! Nothing! Do you understand? Even your precious Zel is another man's bastard!" ' She repeated her mother's words in a dry voice more effective than emotion would have been.

'He said something I couldn't hear and she laughed. "If you don't believe me, ask Clement; he's been trying to forget for nearly twenty years that he fathered that kid, but he hasn't succeeded yet." ' She broke off, then added, 'She knew how to hurt him.' But there was no compassion in her voice. She coughed and put her hand to her neck. 'My throat is dry.'

'Would you like something to drink?'

She nodded.

'Coffee?'

'If you like.'

Wycliffe picked up the telephone and asked for coffee to be sent up from the canteen.

In twenty-five years of police work he had never felt so inadequate or so reluctant to follow a case through to its conclusion. On the way over in the police car she had spoken once.

'When will it be?'

'When will what be?'

'My trial.'

She had asked the question almost as though it were some treat that she was looking forward to and he had answered her harshly. 'You haven't been charged with any crime yet!' She seemed indifferent to her fate; perhaps, more accurately, unaware that she was seriously threatened. He was worried and puzzled by her attitude.

He was looking at her with his professional, blank expression, reluctant to admit, even to himself, that he felt guiltily protective towards her, this girl who had killed two people and tried to kill a third. He would not have felt the same about a man. In this he was unlike Gill. Apart from a passing regret that she was not available to sleep with, the chief inspector's attitude was probably the same as it would have been to anyone else about to be charged with murder, old or young, male or female, pretty or plain. Gill's utilitarian attitude to women made it easier for him. Wycliffe was a romantic; Gill was the better policeman.

A constable arrived with coffee and biscuits.

Wycliffe continued to watch her while she sipped her coffee and nibbled a biscuit, her features calm and, apparently, unconcerned. Had she any idea of what lay before her? The inescapable humiliations of prison life? Her fellow prisoners – would they disgust her? Probably; until with the passage of years she was no longer capable of experiencing disgust or humiliation. Then, when they let her out, still a young woman, would she be like certain other women Wycliffe had known – women broken in spirit, with grey minds, slow-speaking, slow-moving, emotionally castrated.

He thought not. She was made of sterner stuff. For her, prison might be a stage on which she could dramatize herself to impress her fellow prisoners, less intelligent than she. She might tell them her story, but not all at once, letting it drop, little by little, embroidering the theme and so creating her own legend.

Gill waited for Wycliffe to resume the questioning and, when he did not, carried on himself. 'Was that why you killed your mother – because of what you overheard?'

Once more she brushed her hair clear of her face. 'What did it matter to me which of them was my father? She was still my mother.'

'But I don't understand why you had to kill her. At eighteen you are an adult; you can do as you like and your father and uncle would have seen that you wanted for nothing.'

Her dark eyes regarded him. 'You don't understand a thing. I wanted to get back at them almost as much as at her.' For the first time there was anger in her voice.

'Why?'

She made a contemptuous gesture. 'You've seen them! You've seen what they're like!' She looked from Gill to Wycliffe and back again. Never once did her eyes rest on the girl who was writing her words in a book.

By painstaking questions Gill took her through the events of Thursday night. She answered his questions glibly, mostly with indifference, occasionally with impatience. Her answers filled several pages of the policewoman's notebook. Wycliffe sat through it all without a word. His silent presence was beginning to generate a new tension, and from time to time Gill glanced at him, giving him the chance, inviting him to take over. Wycliffe seemed not to notice. He continued to sit, slumped in his chair, staring at the girl with eyes which never wavered. Several times Zel looked at him; she must have wondered why he looked at her with such an unremitting gaze yet never spoke.

He was still thinking about what might happen to her. It was possible that she would not be sent to prison; her lawyers, with the help of their head-shrinkers, would put up a fight. Perhaps they would be right.

His mind went back to the morning when he had first heard of the Bryces. Four, nearly five days ago. It seemed much longer. He had been reading a book on psychopathology and he had made some notes.

'*The psychopath appears to be wholly indifferent to the opinions of others, even to their manifest and threatening hostility . . .*'

Gill ploughed on. 'When did you realize that Irene Bates had been watching from her window and that she had seen you and not your father go into the garage before your mother?'

She was casual. 'I suppose I ought to have known it all along; she sits in that room with the curtains back, sewing, and she never misses a thing. You get so used to her spying that you forget.'

Forget that she is not part of the furniture.

'After she heard about Margaret Haynes she started looking at me in a queer sort of way. I could tell that she was frightened of me, then I knew.'

'What did you do?'

'Nothing. I knew she wouldn't do anything unless my . . .' She broke off.

'Unless your father was involved?'

'Yes.'

'She was very fond of your father?'

'I suppose so.'

'And when he made his statement to us you knew you had to do something. Time was short – you were almost too late – but, luckily for you, when Mr Wycliffe came to question her she was too drunk.'

She did not speak.

'So you made your impromptu plan and if all had gone well, by the morning, this morning, Cousin Irene would have been dead. There would have been an inquest and the coroner would have dribbled on about your aunt being depressed because of the family tragedy – sympathy with the relatives and a nice tidy funeral.'

She was indifferent. 'I suppose so.' She was playing with the spoon in her coffee cup, moving the handle round the rim with the tip of one finger. Gill watched her for a while.

'What about Margaret Haynes?'

'What about her?'

'She was a friend of yours, wasn't she?'

'No.' She continued to play with her spoon and did not raise her eyes. 'She rang me early that morning and asked me to meet her somewhere. I could tell she knew something . . .'

'What did she want?'

'She wanted to tell me that she had seen me coming out of the boathouse with John Evans – that she knew.'

'Was that all?'

'She said that she was going to make a statement to the police and that she would tell them what she had seen.'

'Unless what?'

She was slow in answering, staring down at her empty cup. 'She wanted to make sure that George was kept out of it; she seemed to think the police believed he had killed my mother.'

'She was warning you?'

'You could call it that.'

'And you killed her.'

She had resumed playing with her spoon, rotating it round and round so that it made a monotonous grating sound. 'She asked for it.'

'You hit her more than once?'

'I had to. It didn't work like the first time; she just lay there groaning.' She looked up suddenly, facing Gill. 'I had some loose change in the pocket of my coat with a handkerchief. I pulled out the handkerchief so that the money was scattered on the ground. She stooped to help pick it up and I hit her with the piece of pipe. I suppose I didn't hit hard enough.'

'You had brought the pipe with you?'

'In my sleeve.'

'You killed her because she threatened you, is that it?'

She made an irritable movement which knocked over her cup so that the dregs spilled into the saucer. 'I've told you!'

Wycliffe stood up, flexing his knees to rid them of stiffness. The others looked at him expectantly, but he said nothing and moved away from the table, out of the circle of light, to stand by the window.

It was not raining but the wind swept through the town in sudden gusts, rocking the sign-boards and sending litter scurrying before it. The street lamps on their high swan-necks swayed slightly, changing the pattern of shadows on the shop-fronts and on the road. Wycliffe lit his pipe. Gill, no doubt casting uneasy glances over his shoulder, went on with the questioning; the policewoman wrote it all in her book.

The clock on the wall showed ten minutes after four.

'He is blind to the consequences, even to himself, of his own aggression . . . unable to grasp the idea that his violence may recoil . . . He is totally unable to identify himself with any other person . . .'

Wycliffe tried to understand. Violence always shocked him, though it was so often the raw material of his work, but cold violence aroused in him a revulsion which he found difficult to control. He did not want to believe that it was possible for this girl . . . Zel was about the same age as his daughter, Ruth. Without returning to the table, cutting across her answer to one of Jimmy Gill's questions, he asked, 'Did you have sex with John Evans?'

'What has that got to do with it?'

'He says that you did not.'

'He should know.'

Gill looked at him in surprise. The little

219

policewoman, her blonde head bent over her book, wrote down questions and answers.

'Are you a virgin?'

'No.'

'Who, then? George?'

'Perhaps.'

Wycliffe came back to the table and seated himself once more opposite the girl. He took his time and during that time nobody else seemed to move a muscle. 'Look at me.'

She raised her eyes and looked at him without flinching, but it was evident that she was aware of the new element of stress. Wycliffe looked into her eyes, even leaning across the table as though to make closer contact.

'Why did you tell your father that George had tried to seduce you?'

'Because it was true.'

'It was a lie!'

'Why should I lie?'

'I suppose it was flattering to your pride to pretend that a man of the world like George was attracted to you. In any case you were jealous of your mother. It is not unusual.'

She mustered some indignation. 'Are you saying . . . ?'

Wycliffe went on as though she had not spoken. 'Although George Bryce did his best to let you down lightly, your pride was hurt – and he wasn't going to get away with that; he had to go.' Wycliffe stopped to relight his pipe but he continued to watch her over the flame of the match. 'The psychiatrists will spend a lot of time and a lot of somebody's money trying to find out what they will call your *real* reasons for what you did. They will probably decide that you are emotionally retarded.' He spoke between puffs at his pipe. 'That sounds innocent enough, but three people have died.' He blew out the match and dropped it into the tin lid which served as an ashtray. 'You are going to be the centre of attraction for a long time, Zel. You will enjoy that. Nobody will spare a thought for the silly woman who had the misfortune to become your mother and who died thirty or forty years too soon. Nobody – or nobody who matters – will trouble themselves about the girl – the girl of your own age whom you clubbed to death because she had the impudence to get into bed with a man who wouldn't have you . . .'

He stopped speaking and sat back in his chair. She was drawing her forefinger repeatedly across the shiny table-top and studying the slight smears which it made.

'Of course, in the end, they will put you away for quite a long time and people will forget about you.'

She did not look up.

'Take her away.'

The policewoman sprang to life. Zel looked up in surprise. 'Have you finished?'

'*The psychopath is never a depressive; his hatred is always outwardly directed . . . He has no problem of self-justification and is untroubled by feelings of guilt . . .*'

It was broad daylight when Wycliffe arrived back at his hotel. A damp breeze ruffled the surface of the estuary and overhead grey clouds scurried inland. He felt sick at heart. The hotel was not yet awake and he let himself in with the pass-key they had given him. On an impulse he went into the telephone booth in the lobby and dialled his home number. After a brief interval his wife's voice came sleepily. 'My husband is away . . .'

'I know.'

'Charles! Is something wrong?'

'Nothing. Is Ruth there?' Ruth was his daughter.

'Of course! She's in bed asleep; it's only six o'clock.'

Of course.

'What's the matter, Charles?'

What could he say?

The girl was a mental case; there could be no other explanation . . .

THE END

All Orion/Phoenix titles are available at your local bookshop or from the following address:

Mail Order Department
Littlehampton Book Services
FREEPOST BR535
Worthing, West Sussex, BN13 3BR
telephone 01903 828503, *facsimile* 01903 828802
e-mail MailOrders@lbsltd.co.uk
(Please ensure that you include full postal address details)

Payment can be made either by credit/debit card (Visa, Mastercard, Access and Switch accepted) or by sending a £ Sterling cheque or postal order made payable to *Littlehampton Book Services*.
DO NOT SEND CASH OR CURRENCY

Please add the following to cover postage and packing

UK and BFPO:
£1.50 for the first book, and 50p for each additional book to a maximum of £3.50

Overseas and Eire:
£2.50 for the first book plus £1.00 for the second book and 50p for each additional book ordered

---

BLOCK CAPITALS PLEASE

name of cardholder _____   *delivery address*
_____   *(if different from cardholder)*

address of cardholder _____   _____

_____   _____

_____   _____

postcode _____   *postcode* _____

☐ I enclose my remittance for £ _____

☐ please debit my Mastercard/Visa/Access/Switch (delete as appropriate)

card number ☐☐☐☐☐☐☐☐☐☐☐☐☐☐☐☐

expiry date ☐☐☐☐   Switch issue no. ☐☐

signature _____

prices and availability are subject to change without notice